RANGE WAR OF CALLIE COUNTY

T0243565

RANGE WAR OF CALLIE COUNTY

DUSTY RICHARDS

THORNDIKE PRESS

A part of Gale, a Cengage Company

LIBRARY OF CONGRESS CIP DATA ON FILE.
CATALOGUING IN PUBLICATION FOR THIS BOOK
IS AVAILABLE FROM THE LIBRARY OF CONGRESS.

ISBN-13: 978-1-4205-1604-3 (softcover alk. paper)

Published in 2024 by arrangement with Roan & Weatherford Publishing Associates.

Printed in the USA
1 2 3 4 5   28 27 26 25 24

This one's for Cyndy

FOREWORD

Life is what happens when you're busy making other plans. Boy, did John Lennon nail that particular pearl of wisdom, or what?

I've been thinking a lot lately about life, and old age, and the concept of legacies. Appropriate, when you consider some of the themes my old friend Dusty Richards baked into this particular novel with characters like Neemore Davis, Jed Mahan, and Alex Woodbridge. While Range War of Callie County — previously published years ago under the title Brackeen's Law — is the kind of rousing, ranch-borne western Dusty is famous for, if you read between the lines, it's also a story about how a man faces life, love, and the specter of death as he ages. It's subtle, to be sure. But under the dust and grit, the sweat and testosterone-heavy machismo of life in South Texas after the Civil War, the deeply layered characters and their outlooks on life begin to take on more meaning. As they do, it makes you realize not only what a superb storyteller Dusty at his best really was, but also that he was one of those people who just seemed to get it.

First and foremost, we meet Jed Mahan, a young Texas rancher full of piss and vinegar. At first blush, this is his story. Invincible, immortal, swaggering about with spurs on his heels and a six-gun on his hip, he's the quintessential John Wayne-type cowboy. The smirking bad boy with the heart of gold who doesn't think twice about risking life and limb over even the smallest of challenges. Who of us hasn't encountered this sort of cocky rogue in our lives? Hell, if you're a man reading this, you've either been Jed at some point in your life or yearned to be at the very least. If you're a woman, you've more than likely fallen for more than one, then left them later when they couldn't seem to grow up or take anything seriously. Yeah, I see you out there shaking your heads and denying it, but we all know it's the truth. When we're young, this is who we are and who we always want to be — confident, strong, secure in ourselves, our choices, our destiny, and our bodies. Jed is a young man with a lot on the ball, but he's about to learn some difficult lessons when his stubborn streak puts him and everyone he cares about in danger.

On the other side of the equation is Alex Woodbridge, Callie County's grizzled, tough-as-nails old sheriff. A bow-legged ex-Texas Ranger with a deep voice and a Texas drawl — I picture Sam Elliot in this role — he's seen it all, killed more men than he can count. If they have to grow old, Alex is the guy all young men want to become — hard, feared, respected. Able to stop some young upstart in his tracks with nothing but an Eastwood-like icy stare that says, "Go ahead, punk. Make my day." He cuts a fearsome, distant, almost father-like figure Jed comes to both resent and admire. Alex keeps a secret, though. Something young men don't know, that he'll barely admit to himself. With advancing years comes infirmity. Insecurity. Uncertainty. Regret. Loneliness. He feels age stalking him like a predator. It's terrifying, this existential dread, time whispering in his ear. It keeps him up nights, makes him moody and irascible, makes him wonder what his legacy will be when he's gone. Defenseless as he is against it, though, he refuses to surrender. He won't give in gracefully. If he must go, he envisions himself going out as he's lived, with a gun in his hand and a curse on his lips.

Finally, between the polar opposites of Jed and Alex, we have the character who steals the show — Neemore Davis. Chubby, balding, fussy, middle-aged, and bespectacled, Callie County's mild-mannered county judge is not the person you'd expect to be a hero of a Western. Oddly enough, though, while it takes him some time to get there, he's the guy Dusty uses to bring the entire story together.

Neemore was once a young, cocksure cowboy himself, living down and dirty out on the range and taking life as it came. Then, whether by choice or circumstance, he grew up. He got an education, traded in his chaps and spurs for a suit and tie, got married, and settled down into life as Callie County's most upstanding citizen — dependable, responsible, decent. He's the calm voice of reason keeping Alex's itchy trigger finger at bay, the unbiased rule of law keeping the rougher side of the county in check. Yet, for reasons he doesn't understand, Neemore isn't satisfied. He's restless. Sitting a horse for more than an hour makes him sore and irritable, but he looks back upon his vagabond ranch-hand days wistfully, wondering where they went, and how he came to be where he's at. While he knows he's where he should be — has the right job, the right house, the right wife — he aches for something more. This leads him to resent all that he has and has achieved and put himself in danger of losing it all.

While the collision of these three men is the basis for the primary conflict of *Range War of Callie County,* it's also much more than that. Dusty Richards, the master storyteller, has written an allegory for the battle that each of us fights within ourselves over the passing of years. Think back over your own life. Me? I've been Jed Mahan — young, cocky, immortal. To some extent, I still am. But I'm forty-one years old as I write this in mid-2019, and things have started to change for me. I've slowed down. My kids are growing up, graduating from high school, having babies of their own. When I look at my sons, I don't see little boys anymore. I see new, impossibly young and dangerously reckless versions of myself of yesteryear. Then I look at myself in the mirror as I am today. How did I get here, become the man looking back at me with the white creeping into my beard and the gray at my temples? I've become Neemore Davis — the upstanding patriarch, the husband, the father, the soon-to-be-grandfather, the responsible and successful eldest son. I own a house. I have life insurance. I wear a tie. All the things I swore I would never do. I have "arrived," so to speak.

Yet as great as I have it — that I know I have it — I struggle. I'm not satisfied. Looking back at my life so far, I feel so many things. Regret for bad choices and missed opportunities. Amazement at both my own stupidity and luck to survive it all. Wistful longing for seemingly simpler days where I had fewer worries and less responsibility. How long do I have left? What will I leave behind for my children and my children's children? What can make me happy again, and is it worth risking everything I've worked for to get here?

Now that I'm older and I can actually look forward, though, Alex — while cool in a badass, Special Agent Leroy Jethro Gibbs kind of way — is not who I want to become. No matter how badass it might be, I don't want to be the aging gunfighter who stayed in the game too long because I couldn't find — or keep — happiness elsewhere. Who came to feel that my only exit was to go out in a blaze of glory. If I decided to throw it all to the wind, buy a sports car I can't drive at top speed without risking arrest, forget anything but my own selfish desires, I realize that's the kind of person I would

CHAPTER No. 1

Jed Mahan leaned his shoulder against the doorjamb, a corn shuck cigarette dangling from his lip. He had been watching the sun-bleached, brush-clad hills around the Texas homestead, but there was no sign of Brackeen's men. Jed drew in deeply on his cigarette, then exhaled the biting smoke through his nostrils. He doubted Brackeen would waste any of his men's time tracking him down — he wasn't worth the trouble.

With a wry smile, he turned his attention to the livestock in the dust-covered yard. Four Spanish goats reared on their hind legs to nibble at the mesquite branches. The smell of roasting kid drifted from inside the adobe house and whetted Jed's appetite.

Earlier, he'd been on hand to watch the roasting kid's demise. Gabriella had slipped up behind the small billy as he knelt suckling at his mother. The kid had been so intent on the udder that it had been cap-

15

tured before fear could send it bounding away.

He'd stood by in silent amazement as Gabriella hung the squealing kid by its hind legs in the two hemp ropes that swung from the mesquite. Swinging back and forth, the little one screamed in plaintive protest until her razor cut its wattled throat.

Jed wondered why in hell she hadn't stunned it first with a club. He watched fascinated as she deftly skinned the small carcass. Her well-aimed kick sent a hungry cur yelping to a respectable distance until she completed her butchering.

After she carried the pink carcass into the *jacal,* the slinking dogs hadn't taken long to clean up the entrails. Then, acting sleepy, the pack of curs padded away into the shade of a tree.

But the dogs were always alert. No one came up the canyon to Contres's place without the dogs announcing the presence of trespassers. Gabriella liked it that way. If she was entertaining when her husband returned from Mexico, the barking dogs let her know, giving her guest time to pull on his pants.

Jed wasn't concerned about her absent husband. Although he once heard Pablo himself say, "Someday, I'll catch my little

16

Gabriella in bed with a man, then I'll have to whip the hell out of her." The Mexican then bellowed with laughter and added, "But then, I will have no more dogs, because Gabriella would cut them up and feed them to me in a stew."

He grinned at the recollection. Dog meat wasn't so bad, not if you didn't know you were eating it. He was seldom choosy about his food, especially when he could share it with an ample-hipped woman like Mrs. Gabriella Contras. Theirs was a convenient arrangement since Pablo spent most of his time in Mexico. Her man rustled cattle and stole whatever he needed and, only when things got too hot for him below the border, did Pablo return to his young wife. Sometimes he brought a stolen cattle herd back to sell to people like Jed, who usually put his order in when he knew Pablo was making a trek back to Old Mexico.

However, he suspected the Mexican had another young paramour below the border. He grinned at the thought and smashed his cigarette butt on the adobe wall beside the door, then turned and watched Gabriella set the table. Swishing about in her full skirt and low-cut blouse that exposed a lot of her firm brown breasts, she gave him an inviting smile. With a flourish, she placed the

17

black roasting pan on the table.

At her nod, it was ready. He seated himself at the heavy oak table and sipped a little red wine from a silver goblet, trying to ignore the tempting scene as Gabriella bent even lower over the table across from him. A man, enticed by her beauty, could easily be lured into the high feather bed that Pablo installed especially for his wife.

He'd never asked why the bed was so high. Probably the extra height kept the hogs out of it. Since most of the hogs learned through experience that to venture into the snarling dogs' territory was inviting sharp teeth to bite their shanks, they weren't a big problem.

Gabriella's bed wore hand-carved head and footboards, and the dark oak was polished to an ebony sheen. Nymphs and strange fairy creatures abounded in the artwork. He'd lain there enough to know them well. Regrettably, he did not have time for anything more than her good cooking that day.

"Are you ready to eat?" she asked with a smile as she presented him a stack of flour *tortillas.* Tiny rings of brown speckled the paper-thin bread. She placed the steaming rice and fiery green and red peppers on the table. Finally, she removed the lid from the great black pan, revealing the roasted kid surrounded by bubbling gravy.

"You are not worth this much trouble," she chided him.

The pride in her cooking was equal to her pleasure in entertaining certain men in her bed. She sighed and shrugged her exposed shoulders.

"If that old bastard Pablo ever comes home, I will fatten him up, too."

He laughed as he cut several thick slabs of chevon, then deftly transferred the sizzling meat to his plate.

"Listen to me, you golden-haired Anglo, you'd better appreciate this food," she warned him, although there was a twinkle in her eyes.

"I'm glad that boar hawg stays in Old Mexico. How else could I feast at his table and make love to his young wife?"

The reference to her age brought a smile to Gabriella's face. She gave him a flirty glance as she filled her plate. She was not old yet, but someday she would be thirty. She didn't need to think about that for a while — not if the smiling fool across from her made her feel like a young girl.

He was strong enough, but to rile Brackeen's men was stupid. So, what if Brackeen's men had run Jed's steers away from the creek? The steers would find water somewhere.

She feared he was bringing lots of trouble down on his head to go against the big rancher, Charlie Brackeen.

Her guest was a handsome devil — just under six feet and hard-muscled. The cords of his stomach rippled like tight hemp rope under his light-colored skin. How strange he looked undressed, she recalled. His hands and face were dark enough to belong to one of her own family, but the rest of him was sandy white. When he pushed his hat back on wavy blond hair, a pale line appeared on his smooth forehead. His eyes were a deep blue with crinkling laughter lines at the edges and his mouth held a hint of humor. He was as cocky as a rooster but a very good lover. He did not lose his temper quickly or beat her. In fact, the rancher was a source of much fun and pleasure in her life.

"Just when *is* the *Generalissimo* coming home?" he asked with a wave of his *tortilla.*

"Ha! You think he tells me?"

"Sorry, I won't ask again," he said with a frown. And, especially, he added to himself, if all I get is a sullen answer.

Gabriella sighed wearily and rose. "No, no, Jed. I am sorry." She poured more wine into his goblet, leaning over enough to give him a clear view of her cleavage. "I am worried you are asking for trouble with Brackeen. It is stupid to cross swords with him. Your damned steers can find water somewhere else. You did not need to shout at his men, so they knew it was you shooting at them."

He lowered his head to hide a smile at her ravings. Did she expect him to politely ask those hands to leave his steers alone? Still, it was nice that someone worried about him. He looked up and opened his mouth to explain but was forestalled by the dogs' abrupt barking. They were raising hell, announcing company with their loud, vicious barks. The two of them looked at each other.

"Who's coming?" she whispered.

Jed noted the genuine surprise on her face. Perhaps her husband was returning without telling her.

"Can't you tell who it is?" he asked, reluctant to leave his meal. He waited as she went to the door and peered outside. His brows rose when she picked up the Winchester and cocked it.

"Who is it?" he hissed and stood up from the table.

"It's Woodbridge's deputies," she warned

in a low voice.

"What in hell do *they* want?" He buckled on his Colt and holster quickly, then moved to the other side of the doorway out of sight.

"Hey," she shouted over the snarling dogs. A sudden yelp of pain sounded out in the yard. Obviously, one of the lawmen's horses had planted a kick at one of her curs.

"*Señora* Contras?" a man called from a distance. "We're looking for Jed Mahan. Have you seen him?"

Gabriella's head jerked up haughtily. "What do you want with him?"

Jed recognized the voice of Deputy Blythe. "He's been disturbing the peace around here."

Gabriella clucked her tongue. "That is bad. Well, if I catch him disturbing the peace around here, I'll tell you."

"Ma'am," Blythe sounded uneasy now. "We wondered if that rascal was here, savvy?"

"No rascal here. You go now. I can handle myself good."

He grinned as he watched her calmly dismiss the men.

"Ma'am?"

"Yes, *señor?*"

"If that sumbitch is here, you'd better tell him to come on into No Gap, 'cause this business is serious."

"I won't see him, but I know you are making my dog nervous. You had better go now."

Jed recognized the voice of the other county deputy, Mike Wells. "I think she's lying."

"Cripes, Wells! We ain't going to shoot her to find out."

Blythe said, "Ma'am, you just tell Mahan to turn himself in."

"Yes, I will do that, *señor,* if I see the rascal."

"Good. Come on, Wells, before you get dog bit. I ain't getting off my horse for no damned arrest."

The dogs gradually settled down. Gabriella retreated inside and set the rifle back in place. With her back to Jed, she continued to watch the mesquite and live oak.

"See? I told you, stupid," she said wearily. "You got Brackeen mad and he sent his law to come and get you."

Jed had returned to his food.

"Bastards!" he swore, using his spoon to punctuate the air. "They use the damned law like this was the state of Brackeen — not Texas."

"What law?" she asked grimly. "Now, even you Anglos are beginning to feel the teeth."

A gunshot blasted the air. A dog yelped,

and the mob of curs began a new uproar. Another yelp sounded as Gabriella ran toward the door, him at her heels with the Colt in his hand.

"They're shooting my dogs!" she screamed, grabbing the rifle while he cautiously viewed the empty yard.

"Give yourself up, Mahan!" Blythe ordered from the safety of the brush beyond the yard.

"What now?" She stood opposite him on the other side of the door.

"I'll go out the back way," he whispered.

Then, in reply to Blythe's command, he stuck his hand out the door and emptied the Colt's full cylinders.

"Go," she hissed as two shots thudded into the adobe wall.

"They're out there a way," Jed informed her. He punched out the empty cartridges and reloaded the cylinder.

"Will you go, stupid?" She stamped her foot.

He grinned and winked at her. "I hate to leave you."

"Go! I will make them pay. I think they killed my best dog." Gabriella tried to identify the prone body of the canine without exposing her position.

The deputy shouted again. Jed ignored

Blythe's raspy voice as he hurried for the back door. Dodging behind a tub and a stack of wood on the lean-to porch, be managed to avoid the shot that rang off an iron kettle like a peeling bell. The Colt jumped in Jed's hand in the general direction of the shooter. The dust of another round rose at his heels and he crouched down behind the chicken shed. Deputy Mike Wells was out back, and his Winchester was doing all his talking for him.

Jed calculated the distance to the cedars and brush to be about fifty feet. Blythe was hollering out front, the dogs were still barking, and the hogs stampeded past squawking chickens. A sleepy burro positioned between him and the brush raised his head. The animal would be Jed's next goal. His boots tore across the ground as shots bounced in the dust around him.

A moment before Jed reached the burro, the animal bucked as if stung by a bee. Then the donkey screamed with pain and bolted away, leaving Jed twenty feet to travel without cover.

If he could have spared the time to laugh, he would have roared with amusement. Wells' poor aim had hit the donkey in the rump. Maybe if his luck held, the lawman would have to reload. He cursed himself for not counting the deputy's shots.

When he arrived in the thick cedars unscathed, he was hatless and out of breath, but he stumbled up the limestone outcropping that formed the south wall of the canyon. He could hear Gabriella swearing in shrill Spanish, her Winchester barking from the house. She would be all right.

At last, on top of the bluff unscathed, but on foot, he scowled with disgust. He would have to walk to a neighbor and borrow a horse. He cursed the two lawmen as he climbed a goat path up the canyon wall. They would not dare follow him in the brush. It held too much potential for him to ambush them.

Chapter No. 2

Judge Neemore Davis had been asleep, his steel-rimmed glasses sliding off his sharp nose. When he awoke to the clatter of hooves outside the jail, he adjusted the wires around his ears. Clearing his throat, the bald county commissioner rose and slammed on his pinched crown cowboy hat.

Neemore hated people to stare at his bald crown. With his Stetson in place, the bushy fringe of his hair hid the nakedness of his pate.

At fifty-two years of age, Neemore considered himself a great leader of Texas. While he wasn't a Republican, he wholeheartedly supported President Arthur's policies and took his own job seriously. His was an elected position, but anyone who served in Callie County did so on the approval of its largest landowner, Charlie Brackeen. But Neemore didn't consider himself one of Charlie's flunkies. Although he occasionally consulted with Charlie on local matters, he made his own decisions.

Neemore crossed to the doorway to see why someone had ridden their horses clear on up to the courthouse steps. His answer came as the county's two most worthless deputies stomped in, their voices echoing through the small courthouse.

"Gawdammit, Sheriff Woodbridge, where are you? That sumbitch Mahan gave us the slip." Blythe's voice reverberated across the hardwood floors. Neemore's brow cleared as he realized the reason for the clatter of fast hooves. He pursed his lips and remained in his office out of sight. No doubt Sheriff Alex Woodbridge would want to hold a war council, and he'd send word for Neemore to join them.

He knew his legal knowledge and position as commissioner were important additions to the meetings. He was proud of his certificate from Larken College in Philadelphia, that stated, *Letter of Law and Jurisprudence Is Hereby Issued to Neemore D. Davis.* The certificate came from a mail-order course that Neemore had studied to better handle the legal affairs in the county in the circuit judge's absence.

"Your Honor," Blythe called from outside the door, "come down to the Sheriff's office." He stuck his bowler-covered head through the open door. "We're having a council meeting"

Neemore nodded and tried to appear busy and preoccupied, as fitted his illustrious position.

"Be there in a minute, Blythe."

"Make it soon as you can, Judge. Please. We've got real problems," Blythe said respectfully.

Neemore's lips moved fractionally in a smile. That Blythe was all right. He had a courteous manner that made for good relations.

He sighed. Deciding he'd stalled long enough, he moved down the hall at a leisurely pace and checked his gold watch, then placed it back in his vest pocket. It didn't matter what time it was. The simple action looked impressive to anyone around who might be watching him, and one in positions of responsibility must always keep up appearances. Now, though, there was only Tate Reed, who was serving out a drunk and disorderly charge by using his time mopping the courthouse floors.

"Close the door, Neemore," Alex Woodbridge said absently, barely acknowledging his presence.

"Pull up a chair." Sheriff Woodbridge was

a formidable looking man. He wore a clipped, frost-colored mustache, and the skin on his thin face was stretched so tightly that the veins looked like pulsing worms beneath his skin. The black patch covering his left eye socket added to the ex-ranger's steely appearance. He looked like what he was — a tough, quick-tempered man.

"That sumbitch, Jed Mahan, is getting to be a damned pain in the ass, Neemore," the Sheriff began. "I sent the boys out to arrest him," he nodded to indicate the two deputies standing against the wall. "Hell, you know all that since you issued the warrant. The boys rode out to that Spic bandit's place and they run into a hornet's nest. They damned near got shot up!"

Neemore frowned thoughtfully. That didn't sound like Jed Mahan. The rancher wasn't a trouble maker, but he had shot at Brackeen's men. Hell, he'd just have to pay a fine to settle the matter.

"Was Mahan there?" he asked the deputies.

"Of course, the bastard was there!" Alex answered for his men. "Why the hell else would they have a shootout?"

Raising his brows, Neemore looked from one deputy to the other. "Who got shot?"

"Don't look at me," burly Mike Wells said

defensively. "Hell, we shot a mangy dog, a burro in the ass, and a couple of hawgs. Blythe's the one that shot the hawgs and dogs."

"I just. . . ." Wells trailed off when he noted the tiny veins throbbing at Alex's temple.

The lawman's fist came down heavily on the wooden desk. "Gawdammit, boys! Were you having target practice?"

The two men shifted uncomfortably, their spurs scraping the wooden floor. Woodbridge was not a man to be trifled with.

"We were just carrying out the warrant. Gabriella was shooting hell out of everything with her rifle and Mahan had his six-gun blazing. It was a damned crazy deal, what with the damned dogs barking, chickens squawking, and them bullets buzzing around us."

"And just what in shit did they hit? I don't see a mark on either of you," Alex accused, raking them with a hard look.

Blythe shrugged. "Nothing, I guess."

"You *guess*? Well, I think the pair of you are dumbasses. If I couldn't go arrest me a two-bit rancher without getting whipped by a Mexican whore, I'd hand in my badge and ride on to Ft. Worth. They may need someone there to work the damn sheep pens."

He jerked up and turned his back on the pair. Folding his arms on his chest, he paced the floor, his bowed legs quickly covering the distance to the window.

"But you said —"

Alex whirled and silenced Blythe by stabbing the air with his thin trigger finger. "I said to arrest him, not shoot up the damned livestock. You'll have every Mexican between here and Old Mexico stirred up. Contras might be an old bandit, but he's got lots of folks who owe him favors. Damn, I figured you boys could handle something simple as this."

"Contras wasn't even there," Wells said.

"Hell, no!" Alex swore. "But you can bet his woman sent word for that blowhard to pack his stinking ass up here, because my dumb deputies shot up her livestock."

"Alex is right, boys," Neemore warned. "If old Contras gets enough of these Mexicans riled up, we'll have a hell of a time trying to collect taxes." Neemore didn't relish the thought of his annual job becoming any tougher. The voluntary tax was a misnomer. Although it was not used to fix the roads as the officials always promised, the taxes *were* vital to Callie County. They depended on that money to operate the county government.

Neemore turned and scowled at the deputies.

"See!" Alex said. "We may have kicked over a goldurn beehive and stirred them up when we went after Mahan. He's got a lot of friends around here who could cause us some big trouble."

Wells moved away from the wall. His eyes narrowed as he suggested, "A forty-five slug in his head could spare us all that trouble you're talking about, Sheriff."

"Oh, don't be so damned stupid, Mike!" Alex scoffed. "We don't need no martyr. The small ranchers may think we're out to nail his butt on a cross, and they just might get the idea that he's suddenly saint somebody. Facts, boys. The more we push this thing, the more damned stink it'll raise around here. Just shut up about the whole deal. We'll wait and see if things don't die down some, before we do anything else." He shook his head. "Right, Neemore?"

Neemore ran a palm over his chin and nodded slowly. "Might be the best thing. Just let it simmer, Alex, and later you can catch Jed off guard."

The deputies nodded quickly in agreement.

Neemore shook his head. So, everybody agreed that they'd just bide their time. In the meantime, who was going to go tell Charlie Brackeen that Jed had outsmarted them?

Alex sat back down and sighed heavily. "You boys go get some rest. I'll figure something out. And remember, keep your gawdamn mouths shut!"

Neemore looked across the desk at the red-faced sheriff. Alex was beating a nerve-wracking tattoo on the desktop with his slender fingers. A pulse still throbbed at his temple, almost keeping time with his drumming fingers.

The judge cleared his throat and dropped his gaze. "So, you want to ride out and tell the man?" He glanced out the window, avoiding that hard-blazing eye of Alex's to look across the street in time to see the widow Guthrie drive her buckboard up to Swafford's Dry Goods.

In his imagination, Neemore could hear her shrill voice ordering everyone around as if she were the only one around with any sense. Maybe old Guthrie had killed himself to escape that hatchet-faced woman. He had broken his neck in a wreck when his horse stumbled. Hell would probably be a pleasure for him after twenty years with that harping woman.

"Neemore! You listening to me?"

Turning his face back to the sheriff's, he spoke absently, "Yah, sir, I was just thinking about them boys work for you, so I figure you can go see Charlie this time." He dropped in a chair and wiped at his brow.

"I'll handle it."

Neemore pushed his glasses back on his nose. He wanted everything straight in his mind. If Charlie came snarling at him, he needed his facts right, well ahead of time. "Fine. You going up there this evening?"

"Reckon so. Probably go about dark. You want to take off now?"

He pushed himself up from the wood chair. "Yeah. We just need an official around the courthouse in case something happens."

"I'll handle whatever comes up." Alex frowned when he made no move to leave. "What are you waiting for?"

Gesturing toward the window, Neemore answered dryly, "Oh, that widow Guthrie's over at Swafford's store, and I ain't in no mood to get an earful of her sassy mouth when I cross the street."

Alex rose and went to the window. "I don't blame you none. It's not been much of a day. I wish those damned deputies had better sense. What a stunt they pulled today. When I was rangering, I'd a kicked two grown men's asses for a fracas like that. Yet, those two just let Jed Mahan waltz away, free as a bird. Ah, I tell you, Neemore, I must be getting old."

Neemore studied Alex's profile. There were deep lines carved in the man's lean cheeks, and his hair was almost snowy white. It sure wasn't like Alex to admit to feeling old. Hell, they were about the same age. And Neemore didn't consider himself to be ready for the checker-playing old timers at Wafford's place. It seemed to him that Alex's hard-living past was catching up with him. Young men like Jed Mahan could make a man feel old.

Sighing, he shook his head and tried to find the words to ease Alex's mood. "Hell, Alex, those boys are all right. Cripes, they're both in their thirties, too old for a nursemaid. They just ain't had much experience. Not like you and me. They need someone telling them what to do."

"Yeah, you're right. But, by gawd, I don't know where in hell I could find any better deputies, dumb as they are."

"There ain't none, Alex. We've raised up a generation of worthless, lazy folks." Since Neemore had no children, he felt confident in making the sweeping statement.

"Nowadays, cowboys got to have bunkhouses — they think it's uncivilized to sleep under the stars. And they got to have at least twenty-five bucks a month in wages. Hell, Alex, when you and I were boys, we went clear to Kansas for forty bucks and keep."

"Yah," Alex barked a laugh, "and blowed it all on whores and whiskey in less than a week."

"That's right. We rode home busted, but, by gawd, they knew we'd been there, didn't they?"

Alex's bottom lip moved, almost as though he were smiling. He let out a deep sigh and turned toward the window again.

"That was a long time ago, Neemore. Times are changing. Even the Indians are getting civilized." He ran a finger lightly over his black patch, as though remembering.

Neemore watched him in silence, unaccustomed to seeing Alex in such a mood. He opened his mouth, trying to find some words of wisdom, but they stuck in his throat.

"Neemore," Alex said absently, his thoughts obviously still far away in another place and time, "you go on out the back way."

"I guess so," he said, although he was glad for an excuse to get away. Alex was putting him in a depressed mood. "Yeah, it's a damned shame," Neemore scowled and changed the subject, "when the county commissioner can't even cross the street without dreading some old witch's sharp tongue."

He watched Alex's face for some sign of dismissal. When the sheriff nodded, Neemore checked his watch then pocketed it again. He hoped Alex wasn't stewing about Jed Mahan getting away. Well, there wasn't anything to do about it. Alex had agreed that they should just sit on the problem for a while. Neemore wiped his perspiring forehead with a white handkerchief and turned toward the door, leaving the sheriff to his own private, possibly tormenting, thoughts.

Outside of the courthouse, Neemore swung behind the adobe and rock houses where a dozen copper-colored children were screaming and playing. He moved past them and then behind Ben's Saloon. There he followed the path to a row of six tents. A dirt-packed trail, called Ben's Trace, led to the tents that contained Sid Rourke's girls. No one rode a horse down the Trace. The path followed a high-cut bank that overlooked Dead Horse Creek, but that long hold of water was off limits too. Except for a few black-eyed Mexican children, and, of course, the men who needed the girls' charms, no one came around this side of town.

Sid Rourke owned Ben's Saloon, but he had never changed the name. It had always been Ben's, so Sid left it as it was. As he passed behind it, Neemore glanced at the adobe structure. He knew Rourke would be serving hot beer and bad whiskey, or he would be busy cheating at cards. Since Neemore didn't feel the need for those kinds of pursuits, he moved through the cedar and mesquites, striding up the path which led to tent number three. His need was of a different kind.

Seated inside the tent on a crate with her dress pulled up above her knees, was his dark-skinned lover, Dolores. As Neemore ducked inside, he was immediately struck by the cloying heat and the musky scent of the woman. The sigh of Dolores's legs and small, dust-coated feet brought a smile to his face. The commissioner wasn't sure if her own smile was for him or for the dollar that she knew he would pay. He really didn't care what caused her smile. He didn't feel guilty at taking his pleasure here in a tent. A man fifty-two years old with a wife who had grown weary of love-making had to take his pleasure where he found it. Besides, he liked to hear a woman moan and cry. Josie hadn't done that in some twenty-odd years. Even if Dolores was only acting, he enjoyed her squeals. At least he could imagine he was bringing pleasure to a woman, which was nearly as good as actually doing it.

Neemore wasn't about to leave his wife. She cooked, kept house, and rarely nagged him. This pleasure was a simple matter of a man's need. And that was the whole purpose of having Ben's Trace in No Gap. Of course, there were a passel of folks in favor of burning down the old Army sidewall tents. But those people were mainly the "good women" and perhaps a few hypocritical men. But they didn't fool Neemore. He knew they were only trying to impress others with their supposed high morals.

He undressed quickly, rivers of sweat running down his dark-haired body. Standing slightly bent to accommodate his height against the peak of the tent, he waited for Dolores to shrug out of her duster. One day, he promised himself, he would go up to Austin or Fort Worth and make love to a white woman. There was no use riding over to San Antone, because he doubted he'd find an Anglo whore there.

Running his forearm over his damp brow, Neemore silently cursed the heat. He stood fully upright as Dolores posed nude for his benefit.

Who the hell cared how hot it was, anyway?

Chapter No. 3

Jed knew he was nearing the Allens' spread because his feet were becoming tender as the rocks crunched beneath the thin soles of his boots. His mind still hadn't sorted out the reason for Wells and Blythe serving a warrant on him — especially not when the sons of bitches that worked for Brackeen were the bully ones.

When he reached the wooden framework of the Allens' windmill, the ranch dogs set up a loud chorus. Jed smiled to himself. Brackeen certainly wasn't welcome here. A few years ago, Etta Allen had shot a horse out from under Charlie because he shot one of her ferocious dogs. He chuckled. It must have been some sight with the ol' king himself on the ground, looking at his dead horse and then up at the little gray-haired woman. She told Charlie that a horse for a dog seemed a fair trade.

The Allens were Tennessee folk who ran

stock to the south of Contras's holdings in the lower part of Callie County. Charlie Brackeen's range was considered the north part of the county, but he claimed a lot more. Jed's jaw hardened when he remembered how Charlie's men had tried to push his steers up into the brush, opening his grazing land for Charlie's cattle. As he walked through the dogs, he was grateful that they seemed more intent on barking than biting. Still he was relieved to see Etta Allen appear on the front porch.

"Et," he shouted, "it's me — Jed Mahan. Call off the dogs."

"Oh, they won't bite — 'cept that damn blue hound, and he's off with Sam somewhere. Come on in, Jed." She waved her arm, then went back inside, the rifle in her hand now pointed at the dirt.

He crossed the hard-packed bare ground, then opened the picket gate. His feet dragged with weariness as he moved up the flagstone walk.

Etta frowned at him from the doorway. "Where's your damn horse?"

"Had to leave it." Jed stopped in front of her and sighed. "Blythe and Wells came over to Contras's with a warrant on me, and I had to leave in a hurry."

The small woman looked beyond him

toward the dry brush country and clucked her tongue. "Well, come on in. My gawd, Jed, what the hell they want with you?"

"Disturbing the peace, I reckon. Charlie Brackeen's peace."

"Ask him, he'll sure tell you about his power." She grimaced. "You just never mind about them. Sit down there." She pointed to a sturdy wooden chair. "I'll get you some sweet milk and cold cornbread."

Jed removed his hat and combed his fingers through his damp, wavy hair. He closed his gritty eyes for a moment, then heard the back door slam.

On reflex, his hand went to his gun.

Well, shit.

Belatedly, he realized it was only Et going out back. He sighed, hung his head in self-disgust. All this crap with Brackeen was making him paranoid.

He pulled out the kitchen chair, slowly lowered his weight onto the seat, and propped his chin on his hand. The room around him was large and sturdy, and just like everything else in Texas, dusty.

The deer antlers and the rocks of the fireplace had a permanent stain from the ever-present blanket of grit swirled up by the Texas winds. Even the faded, tin picture of Sam and Et hanging on the wall carried its share of dust.

A patchwork quilt covered a bed in the corner. The dark wood of the foot and headboard was frosted by the invading cloak of earth. The Allens's only child had died of a fever early in its life, he didn't know when exactly. In fact, he didn't even know if it had been a boy or a girl. The subject had never come up, and the only thing to show evidence of a child was the faded, embroidered baby's gown pinned on the rough wall. Jed supposed it served as a reminder to the Allens of their lost child. Unlike everything else in the room, the gown showed no signs of the choking dust.

"Took me long enough, huh?" Et entered the room by the back door. "You must have figured I milked the damn cow."

He waved it away. "No, it doesn't matter. It's just nice to sit down and rest a spell."

"It's a helluva walk for a man who's used to riding." Et's small mouth twitched and a cackle left her throat.

"I reckon it is. Wish Sam was here to hear all this."

Her manner became serious, and she looked at Jed with a concerned, almost motherly frown as she set the schooner of milk and a pie-shaped cornbread on the table. "Tell me, Jed, what happened?"

He swallowed a gulp of cool milk, then wiped his mouth on his shirt sleeve. "Well, a couple of Brackeen's men were pushing a handful of my steers off the creek. I watched them for an hour. They aimed to scatter them longhorns up in the brush and leave the grazing for Charlie's. I had 'em red-handed, Et."

He gnawed off a chunk of the dried wedge of coarse bread.

"Well, what did they say?"

"Say, hell!" Jed scoffed. "I shot a hat off the one that they call Pie-Face. The other one was Red Horse, and he never waited around. Besides, he was up in the brush out of range. I screamed after them to leave my steers alone. I figured it was settled with that. That's been three days now. Well, about nine this morning I was eating with Mrs. Contras, when up come Blythe and Mike Wells wanting to arrest me. Next thing I know they had shot one of Gabriella's dogs. Then the dumbasses shot a burro in the ass."

Et shook her silvery head and wiped away tears of laughter. "Shot a burro, huh?"

"Bang, right in the rump. That Mike Wells is plumb dangerous with a gun. Must have burnt that old donkey, 'cause he went off bucking and braying like he'd gone crazy."

"I bet the poor old thing did," Et sputtered out between laughter. "I can just see it."

He grinned. "Then I set out afoot for your place."

"What happens next?"

"I'll hole up until things cool down. If I can borrow a horse, I'll go over to Goat Springs and lay low. There's a shack up there, and I can wait 'til Charlie calms down."

"Course you can, Jed. Finish your food, and we'll go get you a horse. Sam's extra saddle ain't much, but his grulla is a good horse. He'd loan it to you himself if he was here."

"I'd ride bareback just so I don't have to walk."

"S'pect so," Et said with another smile. "how much is your fine? For disturbing the peace, I mean."

"Oh, they charged Tell-her and Shoat Smith fifteen dollars apiece last time. I expect I'll get the same."

Et's lips were compressed tightly. "Yes, I remember." She shook her head and sighed. "Danged if you ain't a mess, Jed Mahan. But you do brighten up an old woman's evening. I can't remember when I've laughed so much."

47

"Well, I wish it was funnier." He swallowed the last of the milk to wash down the cornbread, then rose.

"Let's go get you that old saddle. I imagine you'd like to get up to Goat Springs before dark."

"Sure would. I hate to eat and run. You tell Sam I sure appreciate this."

"Hell, you know Sam. He's out checking his beloved cows. He might not never come back."

As they walked toward the barn, he matched his steps to hers. He reflected on what she'd said about Ol' Sam. He knew it wasn't true. Other than a little liquor occasionally, Sam Allen was a good husband. He never went down to Ben's Trace, and he never laid a mean hand on Et. Their childless life was probably lonely, yet, they were a devoted couple.

The saddle she mentioned turned out to be a hull, dried and curled on the edges, but the cinch and latigoes were sound enough. It was a single fire rig like most Texans rode until the double clench or California style rigs came into use. He put the blanket pads on the grulla and then tossed on the saddle while Et bridled the horse. The gelding was well broken. He was a short-coupled horse, standing around thirteen hands.

"His name's Archie. Sam had an uncle called Archibald, and he said the horse reminded him of his uncle. So, he calls him Archie."

He laughed. "Then, that's what I'll call him, too. In honor of Sam's uncle."

"You just watch that your hide don't get shot full of holes. Sam will be mad as a bulldog for them worthless outfits getting after you for nothing."

"Thanks, Et. Tell Sam I'll get Archie back to him soon." He waved to the woman. "See yuh."

"You, too," Et shouted after him as he trotted the gelding westward. Standing in the stirrups, the feel of a good horse beneath him once more, he'd survive.

In the last rays of daylight, he rode up a narrow trail. Long shadows from the hills above darkened his way along the boulder strewn creek. Archie was sound and easy to control. Before too long, he reined the horse up short at the sight of the small, flat-roofed, flagstone hut in a hillside notch.

Hand on his gun butt, he looked around. There was no evidence that anyone else was around the place. Dismounting heavily, his sore legs carried him up to the plank door, leaving the grulla ground-tied behind him.

Using his shoulder, he pushed in the tight-fitting cabin door.

He could see little in the dark inside — not that there was a hell of a lot to see. A cot in the corner and some chairs scattered about, one scarred little table. That's all he saw, and all there was supposed to be.

Satisfied, he ducked his head and stepped inside, picked up a wooden pail, and went back to unsaddle Archie. After he turned the gelding into the trap beside the shack, he'd need some water.

Some past settler had built the cabin, then died or left for greener pastures. To him, it didn't matter. He was only interested in it as a hideout. The place would make a good stopover until Sheriff Woodbridge settled his two-legged dogs down.

CHAPTER No. 4

Neemore had on his underwear and britches and sat on the edge of Dolores's cot, pulling on his socks. His nose was full of lavender perfume, and he was filled with weary satisfaction. The afterglow of him bedding Dolores was numbing the edges of his mind.

It felt like his boots weighed forty pounds apiece, and they folded above the ankles whenever he tried to stick his toe inside one. Maneuvering around his belly was another problem. Neemore remembered being flat-bellied and hard as iron. Although he was still stout enough to handle most men, these days he was no longer slim.

"Dolores," Neemore said as she came up behind him, "you sure are a fine woman. Someday you'll be married and raise a whole bunch of little kids, and some old *bandito* will brag on you."

"*Sí.*" She nodded.

'Course, he knew she understood little

English, and talking to her was like talking to a pet dog. The dog couldn't understand English, either, but he knew by her tone that she appreciated him. He grinned as he finished pulling on his boots, then turned around and swept Dolores's duster aside. Gently he patted her brown leg. She smiled, then lowered her eyes. She was one hot piece, and he damn sure hated leaving her, but it was nearly sundown — past time for him to get home to Josie. She'd have supper ready by this time.

After he pulled up his galluses, Dolores helped him with his vest and coat. She gave him another big squeeze against her firm young body. Regretfully, he stepped back and took one last appreciative look. He picked up his hat, then tossed her a silver cartwheel. She quickly scooped up the money and clenched it to her bosom. Well, she was worth it. But now he had a hunger of another kind.

Josie could take care of that kind. At least he'd made sure to marry a woman who knew her way around a kitchen, if not a bedroom.

He strode up the path past the foul-smelling latrines behind the saloon. Under the hill, on his right, some screaming kids played with a burro in the creek. Their energetic splashing looked cool and refreshing. With a kerchief, he wiped his brow and crossed the dusty street and courtyard, headed for his small holding a half-mile west on the road to New Hope. Anymore, he enjoyed the walking. That was a strange thing since it wasn't so long ago that he'd used a horse just to go from one end of town to another. On the long days he rode with Blythe or Wells to collect taxes recently, though, his hip bothered him, and he got damned tired of swaying on a horse.

Thinking about it reminded him of Alex's conversation earlier. Was he like Alex — getting old? He'd never been sick a day in his life. Well, not unless you counted having a bad tooth or two.

Hell, yes, he was tired, he admitted to his contrary mind, but he wasn't ready to be put to pasture like a useless old nag. Let Alex worry about getting old — Neemore Davis had a lot more years left.

Smiling, he held up his head and felt a sense of homecoming at the well-lighted windows of his white-washed frame house. Years ago, Josie had told him that adobe was for Mexicans. She wanted a wooden frame house. So, he built her one. After ten years, it was as sturdy as ever.

When he finally entered the house, she

called from the kitchen, "Is that you, Nee-more?"

He didn't answer right away. He sat on the wooden chair in the entranceway and pulled off his boots. Josie was proud of her polished floors, but the grit from his boots ate right into the shine. So, a few years ago, she sent away for a pair of felt slippers for him, which were now always under the wooden chair, waiting for him.

"Oh, it is you," Josie smiled as she came into view.

He slipped his feet into the slippers. "Yeah, it's me."

"Supper's ready. How was the office?" she asked.

"Hot," he answered wryly. Why did she always ask the same questions every day? He looked up at her and frowned. "The office is the same as it was yesterday, and the day before that, and last year, and two years ago!"

Shit. A man comes home to get away from work, yet, she wanted to rehash the whole damned day. A wife like Dolores would be a blessing if she wouldn't ask a bunch of stupid questions.

"Sorry, I was just trying to be interested."

Neemore lowered his head to escape her accusing expression. "All right, all right,

Josie. If you must know, Alex is having some problems with Jed Mahan."

"Oh, well, come and eat. We've got beans and ham. It's a new ham. Swafford sent it over this morning."

Heaving a gusty sigh, he wondered if he'd ever figure out the way a woman's mind worked. Tell them what they want to know, then they didn't want to know it. He slowly raised his head and looked up, searching her face for some clue. Josie had a nice face for a woman her age. Her brown hair was done in long curls that Rosalina painstakingly set every afternoon. The soft gray dress Josie wore matched her eyes. He smiled derisively. A wife had to look presentable to her man. Especially when that man was a judge.

It was a damned shame that she didn't come to the door half-naked and be so hungry for him that she couldn't wait. Hell, they could do it on the Oriental rug in the front room.

Ha! There wasn't much chance of that happening.

Besides, if he were being honest with himself, he might be hard pressed to do it again so soon, following his little adventure with Dolores.

Noting Josie's puzzled frown, Neemore

stood abruptly and continued his original conversation. "That Jed Mahan refused to be arrested. He shot it out with Blythe and Wells."

"Oh, my goodness." Josie mumbled some disapproval as she led the way to the dining room table. She waited for Neemore to pull out her chair, then she nodded to indicate he could sit down.

Over the years, he'd had gotten used to her social expectations, but he often forgot them. It was galling at times to have to play a part, but when his eyes fell on the crusty golden biscuits and sweet, pink ham, he found the small effort to humor her worthwhile. No smooth-skinned young *señorita* could replace Josie. He had eaten enough skinny *tortillas* in his younger days to know they'd choke him now. The thought made him grin at his wife. *No, Josie,* he promised himself silently, *I ain't ever leaving you.*

"What's so funny, Neemore? Do I have a smudge or something?" She wiped her white hand over her face.

"No, there's nothing wrong. I was just laughing about what Mike did today. He shot a donkey in the behind."

"Really, Neemore! Must we discuss such things at the supper table?"

"No, my wife. No, but they can't say that

Alex Woodbridge's deputies can't hit a burro in the ass." He laughed so hard he nearly choked on his bread. Even Josie's frown did not diminish his good humor.

"Is Mr. Brackeen still planning a picnic for July 4th?" she asked abruptly, pointedly looking away from his flushed face.

He nodded as he spooned up a mouthful of red beans. "Sure. Charlie always has a big wing-ding for his friends and employees this time of year."

"County dignitaries, too."

"Yah, them, too."

She shook her bouncy brown curls and sighed with disapproval. "How will I ever prepare you for a better life? You should eat with a fork."

"Gawdamighty, woman. How would you ever eat beans and get fresh, sweet, cow butter?"

"Neemore Davis, you sound like some old border ruffian rather than a man with a letter of law from Larken College. The duly-elected Judge Commissioner of Callie County should have better manners and set an example for others."

He pointed at her with the second half of his biscuit. "I think only you and the governor of Texas appreciate my title. Well, I love you, but I never even voted for him." Neemore's mouth was too full of biscuit to swallow before his own wit consumed him. The buttermilk by his plate helped wash down the biscuit in a painful lump.

Despite his laughter, he really did appreciate her. A man in political office needed a wife like her.

When the meal was over, he checked his watch, then cleaned his glasses thoroughly with the linen napkin he'd had across his lap. Josie had taught him long ago it was not a bib or a handkerchief.

She began gathering up the dishes. "What time is it?"

"Oh, it's not late." He dismissed the time. Why did she need to know the time? Since all she had to do was carry the dishes out for Rosalina to do in the morning. Then she'd play the piano while he read his law book. Finally, she'd feign a yawn and pointedly excuse herself. She'd go upstairs to that oven of a bedroom to sleep alone and he would fold his book, check the doors, and go out on the back porch to sleep buck naked on his cot. His state of undress must not have bothered Rosalina too much when she arrived before sunup — course, she'd had three husbands and a dozen kids, so, no doubt she'd seen enough bare behinds that his didn't worry her. Besides, she would know that he certainly had no lecherous ideas about her. It wouldn't have mattered whether Rosalina was offended by his nude state. He'd sleep out there through the hot summer and maybe even through the fall. Naked.

Jed Mahan sat on the shack's front stoop, trying to catch a breeze. The heat inside the hut was stifling. Even after dark, the hut was still hot enough to cook in without a fire. He sat smoking a cigarette, feeling grateful to Et Allen for feeding him earlier. There were no provisions inside in these cupboards. No doubt someone had intended to replace them later, but that knowledge didn't help him much now. The cigarette was his supper and the whippoorwills in the brush were his entertainment.

It was strange to think that twelve hours earlier he'd been enjoying Gabriella's charming company and food. Here he was, without supper or a woman — and a fugitive from Callie County's finest.

Gawd damn it all, anyway.

In town, Neemore slept peacefully, hands folded under his cheek. His bare back faced the first rays of the sun — the coolness of the hour should have been conducive to his slumber. But Rosalina had passed by him earlier, since now, she was making enough noise with the pots and pans to wake up the damned hoot owls. He was sure it was her conniving plan to deprive him of the best part of a night's sleep.

Finally, no longer able to pretend to sleep, he sat up. Maybe he'd go in there and shoot that noisy Mexican housekeeper. No — Josie might not appreciate it as much as he would. Fitting on his glasses, he looked toward the barn and pens. He'd get someone to fix up the corral someday. When fall arrived, he'd need pens to hold all his cattle. There were always *vaqueros* around who needed work, so it didn't pay to keep someone on the payroll that he didn't need all the time.

Casting a proprietary eye over his spread, he smiled in satisfaction. His herd numbered nearly a hundred ows, and he had a lot of steers, too — he wasn't certain how many. On the average, it took a calf 'til it was three years old to be worth fooling with, so that meant a couple hundred various sized heifers and steers ranged his land. God intended for a cow to earn her own living and have a calf out in the brush. She'd raise the critter 'til her milk dried up, then shuck the calf off because it was big enough to fend for itself. The following year, the process was repeated, so that, now, he had several different sizes and ages of cattle on his holdings. Coyotes got a few, and the Mexicans ate some, and some of them just died. All in all, though, he had a pretty good size herd.

After he dressed, he went out to the barn and forked some dusty hay to his two saddle horses. They had water in the tank. No doubt it was mossy and tepid, but already the wind was picking up, so the windmill was squeaking. The wind power filled a big wood tank with water. The overage filled the horse tank. He would have to get someone to grease the damned windmill though. The loud squeaking protest was enough to dry the cows up. There was always something to see to. As he walked to the back porch, he realized he still wore his slippers. He sat down on the back stoop to beat the grit off them. The back door opened behind him. He turned just in time and managed to duck out of the way of the wash water that Rosalina slung out the door.

"Dammit, woman! Watch what the hell you're doing — you nearly drowned me."

"Yeah?" She gave him a smug smile.

"Well, next time be careful." He glared,

waiting for her to laugh. As the windmill squeaked again, he winced. "Your man grease windmills?"

"Yes, he does that. You want that one greased?"

He stepped into his slippers. "Yes, and soon."

"He will do it."

"Fine. What's for breakfast?"

"Grits." Her lips below the fuzzy mustache pulled into a scowling line.

"And some ham."

"You don't like grits?" She shook her head decidedly.

"Hell, I bet you ate gawdamn *tortillas* for breakfast."

She ignored him and turned back inside. He followed her, then passed her in the kitchen to move to the table. The plate of food looked cold — again. He clenched his teeth to keep from raving at her — not that it would do any good. Rosalina didn't seem to care if he ate a hot meal or a stone cold one. When it was ready, she just placed it on the table, which wouldn't have been so bad, except she never called him to the table. Maybe it was her way of getting even with him for sleeping in the raw. But that didn't seem likely, because even in the winter when he wore his long johns, she followed the same exasperating routine.

"You got any coffee?" he called with an edge of sarcasm. He heard her flat feet padding across the floor. She never remembered his coffee, but that fact had its compensations — when he did get it, it was hot. At least he didn't have to make conversation with the sly, old, slovenly woman. Thank the Lord for small miracles, at least.

CHAPTER NO. 5

When Jed awoke Tuesday morning, he was still wearing his clothes, and his limbs were stiff from sleeping on the cold, hard cot.

A Sonora dove cooed in a tree somewhere above the shack. Out in the side yard, the grulla snorted in the quiet, first light of a new day.

Inside, Jed's stomach growled.

It was a two-hour ride to Gabriella's place, but he'd have to go there if he was going to eat. Perhaps, he mused sleepily, he could ride south to the Smith's homestead, instead.

Neal Smith farmed in the Fish Creek bottom. He and his two boys, Tell-her and Shoat, raised corn-fed hogs. They used any leftover grain to make whiskey. Neal's wife Mae, a dried-up old Cherokee woman, had once gone after one of Brackeen's men with a sword.

According to Neal, Mae had swung an old

cutlass wildly at one of Brackeen's men until, finally, the sword had struck the horse's ham muscle, cutting it nearly in two. She'd missed the cowboy — fortunately for him, since the sword had been razor-sharp — but the poor horse had to be shot. Supposedly, the reason Brackeen's cowboys were on the Smith's spread was that they had found a calf, which they accused Smith's hogs of killing. Although the pigs had, in fact, scavenged the carcass, the calf had probably died of natural causes beforehand. The arrogant cowboys weren't interested in logic, though, prefering instead to exact some recompense for the calf before having to tell their boss of their own failure.

As Jed walked toward the grulla, he smiled. Seemed Mae Smith and Et Allen had something in common — they were tough on Brackeen's horses.

Jed led Archie up a steep trail, and when they arrived on the mesa above, swung up into the saddle. Riding west, he guided the gelding around the brush and trees, his ears tuned for any new sound.

He soon became aware of an unexpected one.

Someone was driving cattle — a *lot* of cattle.

Jed short-loped the horse westward to

investigate. At the edge of the rimrock mesa, he drew the gelding up. In the distance, a herd of cattle was moving in a southerly direction. His forehead creased in suspicion, and his eyes narrowed as he considered the fact. Brackeen! The big man was pushing his cattle south.

Unofficially, the B-Bar-M cattle grazed the range in the northern half of Callie County — everything north of Dead Horse Creek. The southern area belonged to the small outfits — himself, Allen, Contras, Smith, plus a couple dozen Mexican ranchers. The blatant act of driving Brackeen cattle southward was all but a declaration of open war.

Clenching his teeth, he pounded the torn horn cap on the saddle. Off in the distance, he made out a flat crowned hat. Pie-Face owned a hat like that, and he was one of Brackeen's top hands. Jed nodded to himself. By God, it was time to act. He urged Archie down the slope, keeping alert for signs of other riders.

In the midst of the herd, Jed stood in the stirrups, pistol in hand. Cows bawled for their calves, and clouds of dust boiled up tree high. It wasn't difficult to sneak up on an unaware rider amidst the noise and dust. Luck was with him, too. Pie-Face's back was to him, his head lowered as though half asleep.

Bracing himself, Jed spurred the gelding and rode all-out toward the man. Using his Colt as a club, he lashed out at the other man's head.

Pie-Face never knew what hit him. He sprawled over the right side of the horse and hit the dirt. The riderless horse spooked off, kicking and running through the brush. Jed reined Archie in, then turned him around. The herd continued on southward. No doubt there were more riders somewhere in the trees.

After a careful sweep of the cattle and trees, he decided there was only one course to take — he had to turn this bunch back. His decision made, he spurred the grulla on, tree limbs whipping by as he ducked them and raced around past the herd. Archie managed to escape plunging over a ditch by jumping and landing safely on the other side of the dry wash.

When they reached the front of the herd, he shouted at the lead cows, turning them first west, then back north. Scattering back and forth, the longhorns became disoriented. He was satisfied that the stream was set. He drew his Colt and fired a round into the air. At the first crash of the revolver, the cattle began to thunder off towards the north.

Nearby, a rider, obscured by the dust, shouted across the thundering noise, "What the hell's going on?"

"Stampede!" Jed pulled his kerchief up to keep his face hidden — and the dust out of his mouth. *"Hee-yah!"*

The revolver in his hand belched again. Wide-eyed, the bovines bawled and crashed against each other, their horns cracking.

The cattle drive had been successfully thwarted. And judging by the ferocity of their force, Brackeen's cows might not stop until they reached Ft. Worth.

While the snorting gelding rested, Jed speculated on his actions. Poor old Pie-Face would have a helluva headache when he woke up. He might even decide that it was tough being a Brackeen hand. That would be a win, too.

A rumble from his stomach reminded him of his original plan. Brackeen could just wonder who stampeded his cattle because Jed was certain that no one had seen him.

Neemore had put in the day on the county books — a job that burned his eyes despite the Ft. Worth doctor's glasses. Perhaps someday, he would hire a bookkeeper, but so far, he'd been forced to handle the tedious work alone.

"You busy?" Alex asked from the open door

"No." Neemore stuck the pen in the ink well, grateful for an excuse to abandon the accounting chores.

Alex ambled inside. "I rode up to Charlie's place." He frowned and lowered himself into a chair. "I figure we're going to have some problems."

The judge studied the lawman's grave face and wondered at the man's frustrated tone. "How can we have more?"

"Charlie's out of grass," Alex said flatly, pausing to allow the fact to sink in. "He's pushing his cows south right now."

"How far south?" Neemore dreaded the answer.

"Down the west side of the county. All the way to Dead Horse Creek."

Neemore gazed at him in disbelief, but the expression on his face had not changed. "Shitfire, Alex! That area belongs to them crazy Smith hillbillies."

"Yes, including that ear-biting son, Tellher," the sheriff said with a hard look out of his eye. "You remember when he bit off that cowboy's ear over at Ben's Saloon?"

Neemore agreed with a grim twist of his

lips. He had fined the big lummox of a boy ten bucks. Of course, restitution of the cowboy's ear was impossible, but the ranchhand had lived despite the injury. The cowboy was notched for life, and Tell-her gained a reputation for not fighting fair.

"Cows always did wander down south," Alex said, bringing the conversation back to the original subject.

"Maybe so, but not a whole goddamned herd!" Neemore realized Charlie must *really* be pressed for grass. Otherwise, he wouldn't put Alex and the county commissioner in such an awkward position.

Alex sighed and mopped his face with the red bandana tied around his neck. "Wish it wasn't so damned hot."

"Hell," Neemore snorted, "it ain't even deep summer yet."

"By gawd, it's going to be a scorcher."

Neemore smiled wryly. It was always hot in Callie County. He couldn't remember ever shivering from the first of May until October. He leaned back in his chair and checked his watch. Two o'clock. Maybe a couple of warm beers might help him and Alex get a better perspective of their problems. "Let's go to Ben's."

The other man grinned. "Might not hurt at that."

The judge put on his tall hat and followed Alex outside. The sheriff took his own hat off the rack inside his office as they passed it. His spurs clanged on his run-over boots. Why in hell the bandy-legged Alex always wore spurs was a mystery. The sheriff seldom ever rode a horse in the daytime. Fact was, the ride out to Brackeen's place may have been his first in weeks.

Inside the warm, dim interior of Ben's Saloon, Alex chose a side table and ordered two beers from Sid Rourke. Neemore had known beforehand that Alex would sit with his back to the wall. No one would ever get the chance to shoot *this* old ranger in the back — not unless it was while he was relieving himself at the latrine.

He regarded the lawman thoughtfully as they sat in silence sipping foam off their beers. Alex lived with a tall, younger woman named Dona. She was a straight-backed, light-skinned Mexican, a widow when Alex married her in San Antone. She seemed aloof to Neemore, and it was strange to think that she and Alex had been married over ten years.

Well, if the man liked gummy *tortillas* for breakfast, that was *his* lookout.

"You figure Mahan is going to get a bunch of ranchers stirred up?"

"It's a definite possibility," Neemore answered flatly. His eye narrowed to study two dusty trail hands who had just come inside the saloon. He jerked his head their way. "Who the hell are they?"

"Drifters?"

Drifters, huh? They looked like pretty grim characters. Neemore felt their wolf-like eyes on him. The look did not chill him, but he respected anyone with a mean eye. In days gone by, he would have met their stare equally hard, but age taught a man respect and caution.

Rourke delivered another round of beers. "Those fellows at the bar are looking for someone around here by the name of Raines."

"Raines? Never heard of him." Alex fingered his eye patch, then looked suspiciously at the two men.

"You know him, Sid?"

The black-stubbled face of the bartender drew up into a scowl. "No, I never heard of him."

Alex stood.

Neemore sensed the strain in the sheriff's lean jaw, the cold cut of his blue eyes. The tell-tale pulse began to hammer once again at the sheriff's temple.

"I'm the sheriff here, boys," Alex informed

the two men in an overly loud voice.

Neither man at the bar moved. Tension hung in the air as though a whip had been cracked and raised poised to strike again. Neemore wanted to get up and get out of the line of fire, but he sat rooted to his chair. When Alex moved to the right, away from the table, he expelled a silent sigh.

"We're just passing through, old man."

Alex flinched at the young man's dig at his age. "Time to move on, boys. You're time in my town's up."

Hand still on the bar, the drifter spoke carelessly, "Free country, ain't it?"

Alex shook his head. "Not for the likes of you, it ain't."

The situation looked about to ignite into a full-scale confrontation. Damn Alex and his short fuse.

He wished he was with Dolores right now. At least in her tent, he'd be doing something more pleasurable than worrying about catching a stray bullet.

Neemore cursed.

He regretted not wearing his pistol. Until now, his position as commissioner made it unnecessary to carry a sidearm. But with Alex braced against the two hard-eyed drifters at the bar, he knew his own position was tenuous.

Alex's hand dropped to the butt of the Colt strapped to his thigh. "Fill your hand, or drop your irons."

Cool as ice, the tall cowboy grinned into the mirror above the bar. "We need to talk, lawman."

The glint of steel in the stranger's eyes — it was not one of surrender. Neemore glared at the sheriff's back. Damn Alex's reckless hide, anyway. The old Comanche fighting ranger wouldn't back down. Mexican stand-off. Any moment he expected hot lead to be spitting around Rourke's establishment.

"I'm counting."

Neemore stiffened, his muscles strained as he watched Alex's hand hovering near his holster. The damned old boar was bent on a shoot-out. Just how serious was Alex about counting off? The fact that Alex had placed him in this vulnerable position made him angrier by the second.

Into the thick, leaden silence of the bar room, the abrupt sound of horses' hooves drifted inside. Someone had pulled up out front.

Neemore swerved his head. Now, who in the hell would be riding up to the saloon like a damned stampeded herd? He didn't recognize the rider's voice when the man began shouting for the sheriff. He looked back to Alex, searching for a sign that he'd relent, stand down from this nonsense in the bar.

In the second it took to glance that way, though, Neemore saw his friend's hand move like a coiled spring to his gun. The commissioner dove under a table just as the air was filled with blasting gunshots. Neemore wasn't sure how many shots had been fired, but his ears rang deep inside the drums with the explosions, and the air filled with gunsmoke.

From his vantage point beneath the table, Neemore saw the sheriff's boots still planted in the same upright position, facing the drifters. Slowly twisting his head to the left, eye smarting with smoke, he saw both drifters crumpled on the floor, a swirling haze surrounding their limp bodies.

Warily, he climbed out from under the table and rose, brushing the dust from his knees and sighing audibly. In the middle of the room, Alex stood reloading his Colt in a perfunctory manner. The smoking pistol pointed down but still emitted a small trace of blue trail.

Alex slapped the revolver back in the holster. His good eye had never left his victims. What, did he expect them to lift their limp gun-filled hands and shoot him down?

Then, the tall cowboy's last involuntary muscular effort scraped his spurs across the floor.

His heart stopped, and he jumped. It was as if the cowboy was digging in a horse's ribs to speed him to an escape. Neemore looked at him sadly. The only ride this one would make was the long one to purgatory.

The second man gurgled blood as if he were drowning. Sid doused him with a bucket of water to put out the fire on his vest where scarlet fluid flowed. The water quenched the dead man's final movements. A blank look glazed his eyes.

"Well, son of a bitch!" a tall youth swore from the doorway. When this drew a hard stare from Alex, the kid swallowed hard.

Neemore watched, wondering if the clean-cheeked youth had said too much. The judge was apprehensive, because once unleashed, Alex's temper was completely unpredictable.

The young man cleared his throat and shifted uncomfortably. "Sheriff, I'm here on business. We got trouble at the B-Bar-M. A bunch of men raided our drive this morning. They busted Pie-Face's head open, shot things up, and run our cattle out of the county. Mr. Deets, the foreman, wants to see you."

Alex scowled. "I bet that damned Jed Mahan's behind this."

Neemore heard the words and hoped Alex was wrong. He was anxious to flee the death scene, even if it meant going all the way to Brackeen's ranch — a chore he hated, because of the pain that riding inflicted on his body.

The youth repeated, "Mr. Deets said to get the sheriff."

Alex sighed and looked down at the two inert bodies on the floor. "Tell old Buster I'll be along."

The messenger frowned, and cast one last, distasteful look at the corpses before turning and hurrying out of the saloon. Neemore wanted to leave, too, but didn't want to appear weak or squeamish in front of the townspeople. He couldn't decide which was more upsetting — the news of the raid on Brackeen's herd, or the sheriff's pointless shooting of the two drifters.

More to still his hand from shaking than anything else, he drew out his watch and checked the time. Four-fifteen. Not long until his job for the day would be finished. Maybe tonight he'd go upstairs and sleep in Josie's arms. It would be hot as a damned oven in her bedroom, but still the idea appealed to him.

"Dammit, Alex! All I came for was a warm beer and a little relaxation, and what do you do? Shoot up the place like it was the gawd damn fourth of July." It was as good an exit line as any. Not waiting for an answer, the judge stomped outside and went directly to his office.

It made little difference what Alex would have said in his own defense, anyway. After the drifter's very first words, Neemore had known Alex had marked the pair for death.

Wearily, Neemore sagged into the oak chair behind his desk. Taking a bottle of whiskey from his bottom drawer, he gazed at it reflectively. Alex had been changing for a long while, growing more and more withdrawn and vaguely suicidal. But after today's demonstration, it seemed the old bastard wanted to die in some towering blaze of glory. He was not the type to linger on as a senile old man with a cane and chamber pot. No, it looked like he planned to free his Mexican wife from caring for an invalid.

What was all that talk yesterday about getting old? Maybe Alex wouldn't be able to age gracefully. If he kept taking crazy chances like this one, he would see his desire to go out fighting fulfilled. But by damn, Neemore swore silently, he wasn't taking the county commissioner with him. Hell with that.

Behind the frosted door of his office, Neemore tipped up the brown bottle. He thought once again of sleeping in his wife's arms tonight. There was no chance that Josie would let him share her upstairs bed, not when he was all hot and sweaty. Besides, he doubted that she would be interested in any bedroom activities other than sleeping.

He studied the whiskey bottle. Well, if he couldn't derive any comfort from his devoted wife, maybe he could anesthetize his brain with alcohol.

After swallowing a gulp of the burning whiskey, Neemore checked his watch again. Four thirty-five. The liquor would get smoother, the time would pass quicker.

Hell, it had to.

Chapter No. 6

Even though it was late afternoon, Jed was attempting to eat his first meal of the day. Mae Smith had dished up some boiled greens and greasy pork on a chipped plate. Jed didn't mind the poor quality of the food. When he reached the raw buildings of the Smith place, he'd been so hungry he would have eaten a damn armadillo on the half shell. As he filled his stomach, he listened to the furious roar of Neal Smith.

"That rich sumbitch ain't running over me and my boys! No, sir. Hell, this range is *ours*. If he messes with us, Brackeen will get my rifle up his rump."

"Tell him, Dad!" Shoat stood rocking on his heels, his hands locked on the galluses of his bib overalls. The red-faced youth was growing more indignant by the moment. "Kill the old bastard."

Jed suppressed a laugh. He wondered what old Brackeen would have to say to the boys' threats.

"I've been thinking." Jed put his spoon down and abandoned his half-finished meal. "I've got to get this disturbing-the-peace charge settled. If I can get a group to ride in and back me up, I don't mind going in to pay the fine. But I'll be damned if them coyotes of Alex's are going to drag me in like a dog."

Neal nodded curtly in agreement. "We'll go with you, Jed."

"Good. I think Sam Allen will offer to go, too."

"Hey!" Shoat pointed out the door. "Speak of the devil, and he'll come riding a horse. Here comes old Sam now."

The men rose and went quickly outside.

The tall lanky man nodded in greeting after he climbed off his horse. He beat the dust off his clothes with his hat. "Whew, Jed, it's good to see you're okay. I been riding hell out of my horse. Rode up to that hut in Goat Springs early this morning looking for you. Then I followed your tracks. I saw that some kind of ruckus had taken place, and I noticed a bunch of Charlie's cattle headed north in a hurry. I thought maybe Brackeen had got you, so I rode down here to warn Neal and the boys."

Jed grinned. "Hell, don't give me that. You

were just worried about that good horse I borrowed."

Laughter filled the air.

Inside the house, Neal turned to Sam. "We were just talking about riding to No Gap tomorrow to back Jed up. He hopes to pay a fine so Woodbridge'll call his dogs off."

Neal turned and shouted at his wife in the kitchen, "Woman! Bring Sam a plate."

Sam shook his head in refusal. "I got to get on back home."

"We got fresh greens," Neal retorted. "Woman!"

The silent woman elbowed Neal aside and placed a filled plate on the table. There was a brief, hostile visual exchange between Neal and his Cherokee wife.

Before sitting down, Sam Allen looked around for a place to put his hat. No doubt he was worried that the hounds loitering around the house would chew on it. Seeing his discomfort, Tell-her took the hat and placed it on a deer rack.

Sam sat down at the table and picked up a spoon. "Now, tell me the plan."

Jed placed his elbows on the table and frowned. "If you boys will back me, we'll go to No Gap tomorrow and settle this warrant."

"Count me in." Sam lifted the food to his mouth.

"We're going, too." Shoat spoke abruptly, drawing a frown from his father.

"Yeah, you heard the boy, we're going." Neal grumbled under his breath as his wife slapped a plate of food in front of his nose.

Jed ducked his head to hide a smile at the continuing cold war between Neal and Mae. In spite of the two Smith boys' outspoken manner, they respected and feared their mother. They waited until she had placed their food on the table and retreated to the kitchen before they sat down. His lips twitched when he pictured the small, wrinkled woman at war with Brackeen's horse.

The greasy food settled heavily on Jed's stomach. His belly swelled against his rock-hard muscles, and he felt an urge to get up and walk off the fullness. Good manners, though, dictated that he remained seated with his allies at the table. He appreciated their friendship, and knew there was enough force with these men to settle his problems with Callie County law.

After the men finished eating, they retired to the front porch for a smoke. Except for the thrumming of the windmill, it was quiet. In view of the silence of the ranch, Jed found it hard to believe that a range war was brewing.

Early Wednesday morning, Neemore was paying for his dive into the depths of alcohol in the form of a throbbing head. He sat on the edge of his bed on the porch and scratched his beard-stubbled face. He'd slept in his clothes. Looking down, he scowled in disgust at the wrinkles that were probably permanently embedded in his suit. Without his glasses, his vision was distorted, and the grit grating against his eyeballs just made matters worse.

The windmill squeaked, causing him to flinch. A wind was coming up, and the noise of the pump increased with each knot of power. He stomped his boots on the floor.

Aw, shit. His boots. Ruefully, he realized that he'd probably scarred Josie's waxed floors the night before. There'd be hell to pay in the marital court today.

He rose with the expectation of falling from the dazzling heights of his upright position. On shaky legs, he advanced to the steps. Moving toward the barn, his ears buzzed with the sound of a hundred flies. His eyes burned as if they were slow-flaming mesquite logs.

His first attempt to pitch a fork of hay

drew only a few straws. Disgusted, he gathered an armful of the hay and stumbled to the manger with it. Most of his load was dumped unceremoniously in the feeder. Stepping back, he examined the front of his wrinkled suit once again. Bits of hay and strew were matted on the dusty black threads.

Sighing, Neemore shook his head. He needed to change clothes, anyway, before he went to the courthouse.

If it wasn't for the fact that most of the hay would have littered Josie's floors, he wouldn't have bothered to dust his clothes off. But, as he did, he realized the exercise was a futile gesture, and fearing that his breakfast was growing colder by the minute, he gave up the chore.

The judge straightened up and tried to clear his muddled head. Walking slowly, he made it back to the house and entered the kitchen where he encountered the sullen Mexican maid.

Just who he wanted to talk to.

"Why didn't your man grease the gawdamn windmill? It's making so much racket that I can't think."

"He will fix it," she said, unruffled by Neemore's anger.

"When?"

"Today. He will fix it today. Why do you think you are the only one with chores? If you had a full-time man, you could tell him to fix it and not worry. You are too cheap! You don't have a full-time man, so your windmill is noisy for one day!"

"It's hurting my damned ears." He covered them and glared at her hard, brown eyes.

"I told you how to cure it. This squeaky windmill would not bother you if you hired my Diego, but you are too cheap. So, now you must wait for someone, yes?" She crossed her arms in satisfaction.

"How much does this someone cost?"

Rosalina's eyes narrowed shrewdly. "I think twenty dollars a month."

"Oh, hell." He held up his hands in surrender. "Tell your man to start today. And tell him to fix the gawdamned windmill first and fix it so it won't even whisper!"

"He will."

"He'd better." He spooned up a mouthful of grits, shoveled them in his mouth, and almost gagged. Colder than last night's supper.

Gawd damn that duck-waddling, fat-ass, old woman. She'd done it on purpose — *again*. One of these days she'd go too far, then he'd shoot her deader than a stinking cockroach.

But then he remembered the two dead drifters.

He closed his eyes to shut out the vision.

Another revelation slowly dawned on him. That damned Rosalina had tricked him. She'd been trying for over a year to get him to hire her latest baby producer. Damned if she hadn't finally accomplished her mission. He swore and turned to give her a blasting with his tongue, but she'd disappeared. A good kick in that big ass of hers might be what she needed to remind her who the boss was, but he was too tired to bother. Instead, he sat and ate his cold breakfast in silence. He didn't trust himself to look at her when she brought his coffee.

He sipped his — *hot,* thank the Lord for small miracles — coffee and contemplated the long day ahead. Somehow, he had to solve the explosive problem between the ranchers and Charlie. The first thing to do was clear up Jed Mahan's arrest warrant. Judging by Alex's words in the saloon the day before, Mahan was a thorn in his side he wouldn't soon forget. He feared the sheriff would let that thorn fester and swell until it was like a boil ready to burst.

He sighed again in defeat. It was going to be up to him to help resolve this thing before Mahan's incident grew into a full-scale range war. He couldn't trust Alex to give the boy a fair chance.

Jed awoke, lying on a cot in the Smiths' front room. A sad-faced hound had his nose pressed against his own.

The canine had raised up on his hind legs, his forepaws placed on the edge of the bed. With sleep-coated eyes, Jed stared at the curious mongrel. Although the beast showed no malice in its eyes, he contemplated whipping the animal away, though he feared losing some fingers.

A swift kick from Tell-her sent the pup yelping away. "Damned hound," the boy muttered as he shuffled past.

Jed watched the boy head outside and realized why. His own bladder pressed against his private parts so tightly he felt he would burst before he managed to get to his feet. He joined Tell-her at the side of the house. As he relieved himself, he studied the pink-streaked sky.

Tell-her finished and turned to look at him. His voice was full of uncertainty when he spoke. "You figure we can stop Brackeen from hogging up all the range?"

"If we can't, then we'd better put our stuff in a grip and go elsewhere." Jed sighed in relief as his bladder returned to its normal size. " 'Cause there'll be no one else to stop him."

"Looks like we better show some force or else Charlie will think he's the damn king of the territory. Hell, he ain't that almighty yet. He'd have to hire fifty cowboys to keep his cows down here on this end. You reckon he's got that kind of money?"

"Hmm." Jed considered the question seriously. "Charlie Brackeen knows there's not enough money in cattle to hire that big of a force."

"Yeah, I guess you're right." Tell-her's face brightened, and he turned back toward the house. "Come on. Ma will have breakfast ready. She's got cakes and syrup, so we better get back before Pa and Shoat eat all of them."

Back inside the kitchen, Jed nodded politely to Neal.

The older man nodded back. Shoat nodded good morning without taking his eyes off the stack of cakes on the table. Mae came in from the kitchen with a plate piled high with flapjacks.

"Give that plate to Jed, woman!" Neal half-rose, then thumped a crock jug on the table in front of Jed. "We got some good lick. Hard as hell to find good lick in Texas, but some German over by San Antone made this. It's well worth the ride over to get this kinda syrup. Damn, I've known some good sorghum mill men. My dad sure could make it."

Jed's stomach rumbled at the aroma. "Smells delicious."

"Skimming." Neal thumped his fist on the tabletop. "That's the secret. You got to strip them leaves and skim off that green or else it's as bitter as gall. And you got to be sure and not get it too hot, just steam it a little. By gawd, sorghum making's a damn hard thing. Why, I've bought it before, and it was so bitter I'll bet they wrung it out of the whole plant. Shit, my pa would have skinned our asses if we'd hauled in cane stalks with the leaves not beat off them. I'm going to make some sorghum one of these days."

"You been saying that for ten years, Pa," Shoat said.

"Shut your sassy mouth, boy. I reckon I know when to make lick or not."

Jed was grateful to remain in silence and stuff his face with flapjacks. He thought about their mission today. The night before, Sam had promised to get Clyde and Jubal Peterson to join them, as well. Their places were south of the Allen spread, but he was confident they would come.

Shoat swallowed a mouthful of pancakes. "Are we going to go by and get Sam and the others?"

He nodded. "Sure."

"You boys saddle up our horses," Neal directed. Tell-her grabbed a handful of syrup-saturated cakes and set out the door with Shoat hot on his heels. "Hey, Tell-her! Don't you go getting molasses all over our saddle or the gawdamn flies will follow us all the way to No Gap. You hear me?"

"Yeah, Pa," Tell-her mumbled through a mouthful of cakes.

Jed was relieved Neal had warned the boy. He had no desire to be slapping at flies all day, either.

"Woman!" Neal shouted at his wife as though she were miles away. "Me and Jed need one more cup of coffee."

Mae delivered the coffee wordlessly.

Come to think of it, Jed couldn't recall her ever speaking. Her sharp eyes said plenty, but vocally she appeared mute to her world of men. After swallowing the scalding coffee, Neal stomped outside.

Rising, Jed blew in his own mug in hopes of cooling it. "Thanks, Mae." He tipped the coffee her way. His words drew the closest thing resembling a smile that he'd ever seen on her wrinkled mouth. Then she turned and began hauling away the stack of dirty dishes. He left half of his coffee unfinished, rather than suffer the pangs of more fire on his tongue.

When Jed had mounted, he rode up beside Neal, who shouted for his wife again, "Woman!"

It was a moment or two before she appeared at the door of the house. Neal leaned forward in the saddle and spoke grimly, "Don't use that damn sword on Brackeen's men if they come snooping around here. Use the shotgun. You hear me?"

Jed raised his brows, wondering who in all of Callie County hadn't heard him. He wheeled Archie around and had to sidestep the horse to avoid a collision. Shoat was having a hard time with a wild-eyed young horse. It tried to buck him off, and only the boy's powerful arms on the reins held the bay's chin against his neck. Meanwhile, the horse darted about sideways. Shoat was caught unaware and thrown off the right side of the small, mouse-colored horse. The boy sprawled on the ground, and Jed nearly choked on a laugh at his look of bewilderment.

"Ah, shit!" Neal scoffed. "You clumsy boys couldn't ride a twenty-year-old burro."

"Hell, Pa. We got the broncs." Shoat rose

and brushed himself off, then went after the cowpony.

"This sombitch ain't throwed me yet," Tell-her bragged.

"No, not yet. But he's liable to." Neal scowled at his son, then motioned for Jed to move up alongside him. He threw a scowl back at the boys. "When you two get them broncs broke, you get a rifle from your ma, and come on. Me and Jed will meet you in No Gap."

Jed rode the grulla at a trot beside the long-legged chestnut of Neal's. There was no need to look back, the two youths would catch up eventually. The boys were just out of their late teens, and Jed knew they obviously had no intentions of missing an adventure such as the day might bring. Besides, Tell-her wanted revenge in some small way over his own arrest and fine for biting off that cowboy's ear. When he'd related his own version of the story to Jed, Tell-her showed no remorse and seemed justified in his actions.

Jed and Neal had gone only a mile or so when the boys arrived alongside them. They slowed their mounts with a confusion of loud shouts and "whoas" that caused their father to shake his head in disgust. Jed had to look away before he burst out laughing again. The family bickering and silent war had been a source of amusement to him, and he felt hard put not to laugh out loud.

"Hell!" Neal exclaimed at his offspring. "If you'd been with me in the war, you boys would have been cannon fodder." He looked straight ahead, seeming unwilling to even look at his loud sons.

"I wish we had a damn war," Shoat lamented. "We'd show them damned Yankees a thing or two. Right, Tell?"

"Right."

Neal groaned in disgust. "You two are plumb stupid! The only way that I'd fight another war is when General Ulysses S. Grant drags his blue ass over the Callie County line, north of Charlie Brackeen's place. Until then, I'll let dumbasses like you two fight the damned wars."

"But, Pa, you went to war."

"Yeah, I was dumb once, too. It weren't no war. It was pure-dee hell. I crawled in the mud, fought in the mud, and I got so damned hungry that I finally ate the mud. I seen boys no older than you two with their legs sawed off, and I seen men with their brains blowed out of their heads. I marched barefoot till my feet bled, then I marched some more. I seen death in those Yankee's eyes who charged into my gun barrel. Hell,

I slept two hours once, and it was the only relief I'd had for days, cause the rest of the time I was scared half to death I'd be on that operating table with them butchering doctors hacking off my limbs."

"That why you never talk about it?" Tell-her asked quietly.

"Damn right. I'll tell you boys and Jed here something I did, but I ain't proud of it. God knows, He'll just have to forgive me." Neal spat out a stream of tobacco, then continued with his story. "I had this friend named Landers. Me and him were fighting in Tennessee. Boys, I can't tell you how many battles I'd been in, but that ain't important now. But that one day, I'll never forget what happened to me. It still wakes me up at night.

"You boys heard me say your mother was a widow woman before I took her. Well, listen good — I ain't told many. My buddy Landers and I were in these smoke-filled woods. Them bluebellies were coming off a mountain. We was trying to hold them till our men could get our guns set up on this mountain south.

"Sergeant Miller kept pointing out Yankees to us sharpshooters. We were the best — they'd hand-picked us. We wasn't just some infantry shooters. I reckon I killed or wounded maybe twenty that day. The sumbitches kept coming at us. Landers was ten yards away on his belly, firing and making every shell count. There seemed no end of them Yankees. A corporal crawled up twice with more ammo for our guns, but he didn't stick around.

"I kept waiting for that first cannon round from our guns, so we could pull back to safety. My gun barrel got so hot that if I had touched it, it would have burned my hand.

"Then I heard that cannon round whistling in from behind. There weren't any Yankees on us then, and it was our best cannon. But it landed short. Our own guns had hit right in our midst." Neal drew a deep sigh and spoke quietly to his captivated audience. "When I came to my senses, I heard Landers screaming for me. My rifle was gone. The Sarge's head was half-torn from his body. He was dead. Nearly every bone in my body felt broke, but I managed to crawl over to Landers. The blast had got his legs. There was bone and muscles and some shredded leggings showing. His right foot was just gone.

"He pulled me down close to him and whispered, 'Neal, I got a wife at Wicker's Church. Her name is Mae, and she's Cherokee. My folks don't treat her too good.' Pain was in his eyes, boys, but he was tough. He said, 'My people will turn Mae out. You go marry her, Neal, and take her for your own 'cause you ain't got no wife.' Landers seemed to be asking more of me than he would any man alive. I couldn't even look at his legs.

"I agreed, boys," Neal admitted quietly. "I had to. Then Landers lay back and as calmly as if nothing was wrong, he said, 'Shoot me, Neal.' Aw, boys, I tell you that man asked me to kill him as sure as God's watching and listening right now. He asked me to shoot him."

Neal's head was bent low as he continued. "Landers said, 'Neal, you know, if I live, I'll not have any legs, and I don't want to live without legs. Do it, Neal.'

"Boys, I didn't have me no gun or nothing. I was too weak to strangle him, 'sides I knew I couldn't do it with my bare hands. Well, I must have agreed 'cause he nodded and seemed to relax.

"I crawled away to find a damned gun. There should have been guns all over the place, but I couldn't find one.

"Next thing, I don't know where he came from, but this Yankee officer on a fine sorrel came down the hill by himself. I hid behind a tree, and when he rode past, I pulled him off his horse. Then I smashed him dead on a rock. I took his pistol and went back to Landers. I figured he was dead, but he opened his eyes and looked up.

"He whispered to me, 'Do it, Neal. Use that thing and go marry Mae.' He meant the pistol I had in my hand. So, I did it."

Neal fell silent, looked off toward the horizon.

Jed couldn't look at the others. He wondered if he'd have had the strength that Neal did. It was a lesson for Neal's boys, too. The story had probably planted an indelible impression in their minds. No doubt they would look on their father with more respect in the future.

As for him, Jed had to adjust his whole idea of Neal Smith's character. He'd always considered Neal a simple farmer from Tennessee — a farmer with some cattle, but mainly a nubbin corn crop inside his rail-and-pole fences and hogs outside. But now Jed realized that Neal Smith was a hell of a lot more than a simple hawg farmer.

The men trotted their horses on toward the Allen ranch. Jed's spirits lifted at the sight of the Petersons waiting beside Sam Allen.

"Howdy." Jed dismounted and shook

hands with all three men. They all went through the formalities of greeting each other before he spoke again. "Let's get this over with. You all have things to do. I'm sorry to impose on you, but I think we can solve the legality of Woodbridge's warrant. Then we can figure out how to keep Brackeen off our side of Callie County."

The men all agreed and mounted up for the ride. Everyone was armed with a rifle, either balanced on his knee or lying across his lap. Everyone save Jed, who wore only his Colt .45 on his hip.

He appraised the line of men at his side. They made a formidable force to face Brackeen's courthouse bunch.

He just hoped it didn't come to that.

CHAPTER No. 7

Neemore found his glasses on his office desk where he had left them the night before. Knowing there was no more whiskey left in his office, he propped his feet on the desk and decided to just suffer through his hangover.

When he closed his eyes, the memory of the previous day's shootout in Ben's Saloon no longer consumed his vision. Today, the memory wasn't as gruesome — not like before the whiskey washed it away. Unable to nap, Neemore swung his boots off the desk and stood up. Maybe Alex was back from Brackeen's with some word on who'd scattered Charlie's cattle.

He scowled. There was *always* some kind of trouble he had to take care of.

He crossed the courthouse hall to the sheriff's office. The only man in Alex's office was Deputy Blythe.

"Where's Alex?"

"Gone up to see the man. He ain't back yet. Why?"

Neemore swore to himself. Why? Hell! He, Neemore Davis, was the *Judge Commissioner* of Callie County, and if he felt like asking the deputy where the sheriff was, then that was his prerogative.

Just who the hell ran this county, anyway?

Wordless, Neemore turned and went back to his office.

To think that thick-headed underling had questioned his authority filled him with rage. His job as county commissioner gave him the right to do anything — *anything* — he damned well pleased concerning the operation of his sub-district government.

Neemore steamed silently, cursing the deputy. Slowly, his anger evaporated, and the purple rage faded from his face. He took a deep sigh and started toward his chair.

Behind him, the office door was thrown open, and the deputy walked boldly inside. Neemore's blood pressure soared once more. He glared at the man. A damned closed outhouse door got more respect than the frosted one with *JUDGE NEEMORE D. DAVIS* painted on its glass.

"You ever heard of *knocking?*"

Blythe looked confused, then muttered an apology. Then he suddenly seemed to remember why he had burst into Neemore's office. "You better get out there. We've got big trouble."

Neemore frowned.

"Jed Mahan has a whole damn army out there." He jabbed a thumb toward the street.

"What does he want?"

"Damned if I know, Your Honor." Blythe shrugged, looking at Neemore expectantly as if the matter now rested completely with him.

Neemore moved to the window and cautiously peered outside. Lined up across the street was an army of riders, each one on horseback and armed with a rifle.

In the middle sat Jed Mahan.

"Holy shit!" Neemore looked around for Blythe, who had disappeared. "Blythe, where are you?"

"I'm in the sheriff's office."

"Well, get your ass back in here."

Blythe ambled back across the hall. He looked defensively at Neemore's scowling face. "I just figured I could hold them off from in there."

"Go out there and see what the hell they want!"

"Me?"

"You're the sheriff when he ain't here.

Now go on!" Blythe seemed to grow taller as he considered his elevated position. He squared his shoulders and grinned, then swaggered down the hallway to the open door.

"Shit," Neemore swore again and followed. Now the dumbass thought he was the sheriff.

At the threshold, Blythe stopped and bellowed, "What the hell do you bastards want?"

Neemore cringed at the total lack of tact. "My gawd. You stupid-ass! There's only two of us, and there must be a dozen of them. Have you lost your good sense? We ain't in no shape to fight off that army, not unless you're ready to die. I sure as hell don't plan on it. I just want to know what they want — not kick asses. They could cut us to ribbons."

"Oh. Oh, yeah, I reckon so."

Swallowing back his impatience, Neemore spoke slowly, "Now, go try it *again*."

He pushed the deputy toward the door once more.

For once, the moron followed directions. "What — do — you — want?"

"Judge Davis," Jed said curtly.

Blythe looked over his shoulder at Neemore.

"They want *you*," he pointed back at the line of armed men.

"What for?" Neemore kept his voice low, then disgusted at his own cowardice, he raised his voice a decibel. "Ask them why."

"Ah — why do you want to see him?" Blythe shouted.

Jed sighed loudly and shifted on his horse. "Tell Davis we ain't here for any trouble unless y'all start it. We want to see the judge on business. That's all."

Neemore heard the words and cursed under his breath. Where the hell was gun-happy Alex when you needed him? That old bastard shot drifters 'cause he didn't like their looks, yet, when there was real trouble, he was nowhere to be found.

With a disgusted growl, Neemore signaled to Blythe to move inside the door. "Tell them to wait a minute, please."

Blythe leaned his head out the door. "Ya'll wait here just a minute."

When Neemore groaned, Blythe stuck his head out the door and added, "Please." The addition sent a ripple of laughter down Jed's line of men.

It was difficult to ignore the men's amusement at the expense of the county officials, but Neemore managed to quell his nervousness at their mocking sounds. "Blythe, go get some rifles and be ready to mow them down if they get me."

"If they *get* you?"

"Yes. If they shoot *me, you* get *them.* Understand?"

"Sure, sure. But, Judge, what will we do?"

"Who do?"

Blythe shook his head grimly. "If they get you, we won't have a judge."

"Good thinking." Neemore nodded, deciding to humor the incompetent deputy. He grimaced behind the man's back as he pushed him toward the sheriff's office.

Drawing a deep breath, Neemore checked that his hat was securely on his head, then stepped outside. He did not immediately look at the formidable force arrayed before him. Instead, he took his gold watch from his pocket and looked down at the face. Appearances had to be maintained.

It was eleven-twenty.

Slowly he raised his head and moved toward the men who were still mounted, smiling politely. "Gentlemen. Good day. Jed, good to see you. What can I do for you?"

Jed cleared his throat, kept his voice level. "We came in peace, Judge. It's about the warrant against me for disturbing the peace.

I ain't guilty, but I'm willing to pay my fine."

The silence seemed to weigh heavy in the mid-morning air as the army of men anxiously awaited Neemore's response.

"And?" Neemore turned his head slightly, then realized he still held his watch. He snapped the case shut and placed it back in his vest pocket.

This caught the younger man off guard. "Well, um . . . how much is my fine?"

The judge looked up to meet Jed's gaze. "Ten dollars."

"Fine." Jed drew the money out of his shirt pocket, bitted his horse out in the street, and handed it to Neemore.

"This is county money," Neemore assured him with a nod, just in case there was a question about the disposition.

Jed leaned forward on the grulla and spoke with grim determination. "Now. I want warrants drawn on two men who work for Charlie Brackeen. One's name Pie-Face, and the other is Red . . . somebody. The warrant's for disturbing the peace. If there's a trial, I'll be there to testify."

"Oh, yes, we'll need you to testify if there's a trial."

Sam Allen spoke up. "Judge Davis?"

"Yes?" The commissioner turned and

looked down the line until he found Allen.

"We'll all come to the trial." Sam made it sound like a warning. "All of us."

"Yes, well . . . it may not be necessary." Neemore laughed nervously, anxious to end the confrontation. He felt like General Custer must have felt at the battle with the Sioux.

"Judge, one more thing." Jed lowered his voice. "I'm asking you with all due respect, man to man. Don't you send those clowns of Woodbridge's out to arrest me — or any of us — ever again, or they'll come back over a saddle. If you want me for something, come talk to me. Do we understand each other?"

Neemore forced himself to hold the lad's hard-eyed stare. "Yes, Jed. I understand perfectly."

"Another point, Judge. Charlie Brackeen better keep his cattle in the north half of Callie County, or there'll be war. Tell him."

"Fellows, I'll tell him." Neemore shrugged and held out his hands. "But range is range. Charlie's been here forever."

"Listen, sir . . . you just tell him. Tell him, and if he don't listen, we'll handle it ourselves."

The rows of "yeahs" that punctuated Jed's statement caused Neemore to chill in the hot sun.

A shot fired, and a glass window behind Neemore shattered. He swallowed and closed his eyes.

"Now?" Blythe shouted.

"No, you fool!" Neemore screamed, jerking his hands up toward the sky. "No! No! Don't shoot."

But his warning came too late. In reply to Blythe's first shot, rifles blazed. The judge fell prostrate on the ground, covering his head with his hands. When all rifles had fired one volley, the street fell silent. The acrid smoke and dust in his mouth choked Neemore as he rose, coughing. The line of horses shuffled and snorted.

He brushed off his suit, then looked up.

The whole line was intact. Not one man even wounded.

Slowly, Neemore turned toward the courthouse and roared, "Blythe! You're a gawd damned *idiot*."

A small subdued voice answered, "Sorry, Your Honor."

Neemore gritted his teeth, then turned and shook his head at Jed in apology. A look of understanding passed between them.

The young rancher signaled his army, and the men rode out single file. They had been prepared to meet force, Neemore realized.

He couldn't believe Charlie was going against these tough men.

The hell of it was, the range war was just beginning. Charlie Brackeen was not a man accustomed to giving up without a fight, and Jed Mahan's army made a formidable opponent.

When the ranchers had ridden out of sight, Neemore looked back at the courthouse. Both glass windows had been destroyed by the gunshots. Shaking his head in disgust, he decided to go to Ben's for a well-deserved beer. If he went back to the courthouse right now, he'd kill Blythe with his bare hands.

Maybe it was a good thing Alex had been out of town. That old one-eyed Comanche killer would only have caused more trouble. On the other hand, it might be a good idea to turn Alex loose on Blythe for damn near getting the county judge shot.

At the saloon, Neemore ate a lunch of pickled hard-boiled eggs washed down with warm beer. He was resolved not to go back to the courthouse until he was satisfied Alex's chief deputy had gone home.

It would save Callie County a hanging — the hanging of their own elected commissioner for strangling an officer of the court by the name of Blythe Dumbass.

The judge signaled Rourke over, then ordered another beer with a shot of whiskey to steady his nerves. Four or five Mexican customers were watching him fearfully. Obviously, they had witnessed the encounter in the street and were impressed by his confrontation with Jed's army.

Eventually, Neemore called one of the men over, then sent him to check on Blythe. A few minutes later, the Mexican returned, his *sombrero* respectfully in his hand.

"The deputy is unhurt."

"Fine, *amigo,*" Neemore nodded. He ordered beers for the messenger and his friends. With a smile he acknowledged their thanks.

Studying the bottom of his glass he pursed his lips and sighed. Maybe he'd go out back and visit Dolores. To hell with the county government. The whole damned place could fall for all he cared. The sheriff was gone when he was needed, and Brackeen was pushing his luck moving his cattle on those ranchers' lands. Hell, it wasn't worth the aggravation and risks a judge had to put up with.

Perhaps Dolores could make him forget about all the frustration and troubles of his job. Whiskey wasn't the answer, he conceded — not in the quantities that he had tried the day before. At least lavender perfume didn't give him a hangover.

When he reached Dolores's tent, however, he discovered she was already occupied. The grunts and groans emitting from the canvas-covered room caused Neemore a moment of sadness. He stood in the shade and shook his head. There was no sense in waiting around. He peered through the leaf-filtered shade at the sky, then walked back toward the courthouse.

Tomorrow would have to be an easier day.

CHAPTER No. 8

As the ranchers rode from No Gap on Wednesday afternoon, Jed remained silent, mulling his problems over in his mind. There were several alternatives to prevent Charlie Brackeen from taking over their range, but none seemed plausible at the moment. He reviewed and discarded plan after plan. Weighing up a possibility, he turned his head toward Neal.

About that time, Smith rode alongside him. "We need to pay someone to stay up on Dead Horse Creek. They'll need to ride it for a 'dead line.' If Brackeen tries anything, our lookout can ride back and warn us. If that happens, we can go turn the cattle back.

"One or two of us would be helpless, but all of us together like back there in town will make a real force and have a fighting chance."

The older man nodded in agreement. He

looked over his shoulder and spoke to his son. "Shoat, you're the man for the job." He turned back to Jed and smiled dryly. "He's been about to wet his pants wanting war so bad. He can go up to Dead Horse Creek and keep an eye out for Brackeen's next move."

Jed glanced back at the boy's eager face. "I'll put in ten dollars to pay for pay and provisions."

The Petersons and Sam Allen agreed to chip in. Jed was encouraged by their support.

"We can provide his grub." Neal shook his head. "Now the only problem we got is keeping the boy from shooting up the whole dang countryside."

"Aw, Pa. I didn't start that gun brawl in town."

Jed held the grulla back and fell in beside the boy. "Use the Goat Springs shack. And mind your pa. We all need to stand together when we go against Brackeen, so don't try taking him or his men alone."

"Yes, sir."

Tell-her let out a disgusted sigh. "It'll get you out of all the damned work at home."

Jed's lips twitched as he listened to the siblings arguing. Things looked much better than they had a week ago. He was relieved that the matter of his warrant was settled. Talk about a load off his mind. There was no reason for Alex to send his stupid deputies after him again.

He shook his head again in thoughtful amusement. That idiot Blythe was lucky to be alive.

It was amazing no one had gotten hit. And poor old Neemore. Jed almost chuckled out loud as he recalled the scene. The judge had flattened himself on the ground like a damned snake. He'd messed up his nice suit and everything. Hell, he'd probably kill that damned deputy.

The men reached a fork in the road. Jed looked down at the grulla he rode, then turned to Sam Allen. "Sorry, Sam. I'll bring Archie home in a day or so."

"Don't worry 'bout it, Jed."

"I appreciate it." Jed reined in the horse. "Thanks for today, boys. I enjoyed it. If you need me, I'll be around the Contras place." He grinned as the men cheered and gave him a knowing glance. He waved goodbye and set Archie in a trot toward Gabriella's.

As he moved northward through the cedars, mesquites, and live oaks on the winding set of ruts, Jed let his imagination wander to Gabriella. She would be so pleased to see him, she'd fix him one of her delicious dinners. Mae Smith had given him his last food, and to a man who was starving and on the run from the law, it had not been bad. To a free man, though, it would have been slick and greasy. Still, the Smiths were good people.

Archie's hooves clattered over the dry land. Jed wiped his forearm over his face and scanned the landscape ahead. It was dry for early summer. South Texas was usually dry this time of year, but he couldn't remember the last time it had rained. Each day had grown warmer and clouds from the distant Gulf became thinner and thinner, with no promise of thirst-quenching rain for the parched land. He shrugged philosophically. He couldn't do anything about the weather, and there was no sense worrying about something he had no way of controlling. His spirits lifted as he began to recognize the landmarks that told him he was near Gabriella's place.

The dogs began barking as soon as they spotted him. Jed looked beyond them to the adobe house. Gabriella stood in the doorway, her hands perched on her hips.

Jed dismounted and waded through the dogs and bleating goats. A nanny wearing a noisy bell bolted, her udders flapping. Atop the roof of a small shed, a bearded billy gave him a curious stare. A burro even brayed a homecoming — maybe even the one that had taken a bullet in the rump for him.

"Hey! It's me." Jed laughed and held out his arms.

Not moving from her position, she scowled at him. "You are very dirty. You were gone for days." She eyed him coldly. "You leave me alone to fight your wars, then come back with open arms. Here is your lover, dumb woman. *Ha!*"

Jed raised his brows, surprised at her mood. "Ain't you even a little bit glad to see me?"

"Should I be?"

"Yes."

A smile broke out on her face as her resistance melted. Laughing, she rushed forward into his arms. His lips met hers and melted into her sweet, eager mouth. At last, she tried to push him away, then beat at his back with her fists.

Jed stepped back and frowned in puzzlement.

"You will go take a bath and have a shave. You cut up my face with those whiskers. I am not going to make love with a billy goat." She pushed him toward the rear of the house. "Take off your clothes. I will get you some clean ones. My, you smell bad."

Jed unbuttoned his shirt as he crossed the tiled floors. He watched her hips sway as she moved ahead of him. The tempting sight caused his blood to pump faster, and he recalled the vision of her without clothes. He was suddenly anxious to get through his bath.

The water in the wooden tub was tepid but refreshing. Gabriella wielded the straight razor competently as she moved his head with her other hand. The process would have been a relaxing experience, but Jed felt irritated by her pushy manner. Gabriella surveyed her work critically and ran her palm over his smooth, lean cheeks. "I think you are done."

"Thanks. Get me a towel, Gabby."

She looked at him and frowned. "So what did you do about Woodbridge?"

Something in her voice puzzled him. It wasn't like Gabriella to be so nagging. He splashed water over his chest as he answered. "We all went to town — me, the Smiths, Sam Allen, and the Petersons. We just rode in, I paid my fine, then we rode out."

"Just like that?" She snapped her fingers in the air.

His lips twisted, and he cocked a brow at her. "Well, we all had our guns."

117

"Oh." She nodded, then turned away. As he watched her go, a feeling of unease settled in his gut.

When she returned, she carried two flour sack towels. She avoided his eyes when she spoke again. "Later, I have something for you to do."

"The windmill quit?" He stepped out of the tub and began drying himself.

"No," she said curtly, then left the room again.

Sighing, he donned the clean clothes she'd laid out for him. Gabriella definitely had a burr under her saddle about something. Maybe she had word that old Contras was returning.

If that was the case, he would just ride on home. He felt frustrated to see her so out of sorts when he had other, more pleasurable things on his mind. There were drawbacks to everything, he supposed, and Gabriella had her faults. But when one enjoyed a ripe woman like this fiery Mexican, the compensations were worth the occasional snags.

"Come, Jed," she called from the kitchen. "I have some food ready."

He smoothed his hair with his fingers and stepped toward the kitchen. At the threshold he paused and looked at her. She was wearing a colorful skirt and a low-cut white blouse that exposed her cleavage. Her long, raven hair hung down her back in a thick braid. Jed wondered why the old *bandito,* Pablo, stayed below the border so much when he had someone like Gabriella to come home to. Surely Pablo must have known his wife was not the kind of woman to leave alone.

He took a chair at the table. "I think Pablo must be coming home."

She turned from her stance in front of the cast iron stove. Her frown and the slight shake of her head indicated he had missed his guess.

Well, if Pablo wasn't coming home, then what the hell was her problem?

What had her so damn upset, then? Jed stifled a sigh of exasperation and picked up a flour tortilla. Gabriella plunked a pan of beans on the table and snorted softly. "If that old *bandito* of mine came home, it would probably rain. No chance."

He smiled at her sarcasm. He bit into the bean-filled tortilla, savoring the spicy flavor. He would not trade Gabriella's cooking for the silent Mae Smith's in a thousand years. Jed sent his favorite cook a grateful smile.

"What is with you?" she demanded suspiciously. "You are like some crazy man going around grinning."

"I thought you were glad to see me."

"I am."

Thumping his hand on the table, he scowled at her. "You sure as hell don't act like it. I ain't some kind of carcass that them damned dogs dragged in." He was tired of her hot and cold attitude, and he resumed his meal in silence.

It saved arguing with her. Besides, Charlie Brackeen still weighed heavily on his mind. He knew the big rancher wasn't going to ignore his cattle being stampeded and his ranch hands harassed. His eyebrows drew together in speculation. No doubt the warrant had been issued at Charlie's command, because he had gotten in the old man's way when they began pushing the cattle to the south. It was frustrating to worry what the big rancher's next move would be.

Gabriella broke into his thoughts. "You will need to stay at your ranch for a few weeks."

"So, Pablo *is* coming." He pointed at her with his *tortilla.*

"No. I need your help."

"You said that before." He grew impatient with her vague hints. "I'm going to do it now."

"Here." She handed him a large spoon.

What the hell was she up to? He tapped

the table with the spoon as he waited. Gabriella placed a can on the table.

His nose wrinkled at the strong smell of turpentine. "What am I supposed to do with that?"

"I will show you. Pour some into the spoon." She pointed, then wiggled the blouse over her head.

"Hold the spoon under my naval, but don't touch me. Just that far." She indicated a few inches with her fingers.

Placing her hands on the table, she stretched out her body. "Be careful, that stuff can blister me."

"What are we doing here? Is this some kind of witchcraft?" he asked, feeling foolish.

"No." She looked around at him. "I am losing a baby."

His head jerked up and the spoon shook in his hand. "You're *what?*"

"Hold the spoon down there, but be careful."

His mind turned to exasperation. A few minutes ago, he had simply felt foolish, but now he grew angry. What was this crazy woman involving him in? "Why don't you get old Pablo to do this?"

"Is the spoon empty?" She peered at him sideways.

"Well, I'll be damned." He blinked his eyes as he looked at the empty spoon. "Where the hell did it go?"

"Inside me. Put some more on the spoon."

"You mean the turpentine went up inside you?"

Gabriella clucked her tongue. "Put some more on the spoon, Jed."

He banged the table with the spoon. "Why the hell don't you get Pablo to do this?"

Shaking her head, she answered with bitterness in her voice. "He won't do it. He is Catholic. Now, will you fill the gawdamned spoon?"

"Ain't *you* Catholic?"

Muttering under her breath, she arched her back in anger. "I don't go to church and confess my sins." She shook her bare breasts and slightly rounded stomach. "That old hypocrite would never do this. He always goes to the *padre* and asks to be forgiven for shooting peons. 'Father, I have sinned. Forgive me.' "She mimicked in a whining voice.

Avoiding her eyes, he rose and stood back from the table. "I'm leaving."

"Why?" Then she realized she was naked from the waist up and hurriedly swept up her blouse to cover herself. "I will stop. Don't go, Jed."

"You don't need me to murder this thing inside you," he growled, feeling sick at the realization of what she was trying to do. He felt a need to get out of the room quickly. There was something ugly in the house now. He needed to get away — to be alone.

Although he had just taken a bath, he felt dirty again. Not looking back at her, he hurried out of the house, not stopping until he reached the corral. She called to him as he put his own saddle on his own horse.

He couldn't answer — what was there to say? It was nearly dark, but the twilight held no dangers for him. The threat seemed to be here on this small homestead. The whole ugly incident filled him with an inexplicable uneasiness, and he was anxious to escape.

"Jed, I am sorry. I should not have asked you. Come back." She lapsed into Spanish, the words unclear to him, but her tone was one of remorse. "Will you come back again, Jed?"

"You have a man." He gave the stirrup a jerk down from across his saddle seat. He studiously avoided her eyes, not trusting himself.

"Fine! Go away!" Gabriella screeched. "See if I care. I will probably die tonight. You do not care. You are a bigger ass than Pablo!"

Jed stepped in the stirrup, grateful to be back on his own mount. The bay had obviously returned on his own after Blythe and Wells finished shooting up the Contras place.

He glanced over his shoulder for one last look at her. Her hands were perched on her hips again, her head thrown back defiantly. No, she wouldn't die. She was too strong to succumb to the death of the baby inside her belly. He untied the grulla and pulled it behind him as he rode through the trees up toward the steep trail he'd used on foot the day Woodbridge's deputies came to arrest him.

"Go! Go, you son of a bitch! I *loved* you!" Gabriella screamed after him. Her voice echoed in the growling darkness, the dogs joined her baying mournfully. Feeling a twinge of guilt, Jed guided the bay up the valley. He led Archie behind him, keeping the pace slow as he thought about what had just taken place.

He had enjoyed her body as if it belonged to him. Never had he left her in anger.

Stars sprinkled the night sky and shed a silver light in the shadowy mesquite, cedar, and live oak. He felt undecided whether to ride down to his place or to go up to Billy Goat Springs. Surely Shoat could not get into much trouble his first night at the rock hut.

Having decided to ride home, Jed crossed Pinto Creek and dropped the horses into a lope on the dark road. He reined up on the rise and studied the silhouette of his small ranch. The windmill and the outline of the house were all he could make out in the gloom. The closer he drew, the more his muscles tensed and felt edgy for some unaccountable reason.

Ordinarily, he would have ridden in at a gallop, burst into the house, and after lighting a lantern, put up the horses. The trouble was these were not ordinary times, and even normal actions had to be approached warily. There was probably nothing wrong, but still, he took the precaution of untying the rawhide thong that kept his Colt in his holster.

Slowly, he approached the house. The hair on his neck bristled. He was half out of the saddle when the orange flame of a pistol shot sent him into a dive for the ground. Two or three more shots splintered the picket yard fence about his head.

His fist squeezed the pistol grip and lay ready to shoot towards the corner of the house. At the first shot, both horses had run off into the darkness.

A second gun suddenly cut loose, splintering more pickets just above him. He lay flat on the warm, gravelly ground. He grimaced and blew out a mouthful of dust as quiet as he knew how. So, now he knew there were at least two ambushers. He strained his ears. A spur rowel clanged, indicating the position of the second bushwhacker.

He drew his left arm up his side, then used both hands to point the Colt at a spot chest-high at the corner of the house. He cocked the hammer and strained his eyes to see the front sight blade, then squeezed off a shot. In the same instant, he rolled over and over, out of the path of return fire.

Someone shouted, but the voice was unrecognizable. More shots blasted at the site where he had been. He fired his own gun again. In a second, Jed was on his feet and running. If he could make it to the framework of the water tank, it would offer some cover.

The ambushers began cussing, and he felt better. His plan had worked — they had emptied their guns firing at him. Out of breath, he reached the water tank's security.

A rare, steady, night wind was operating the noisy windmill. The snipers' cursing was too far away to be deciphered, or else they'd shut up. Regretting the slap and squeak of the mill, he knelt behind a large post. There were four more shots in his Colt, and he wanted them to count.

The wind grew weaker until finally all Jed could hear was the buzzing night insects. There was not a whisper to indicate the ambushers were still around. He cocked his head and listened intently to the silence. Maybe the men had gone. Obviously, they had been waiting for him on the off chance he would come home.

Holstering his Colt, a sudden thought struck Jed. What if they had gone to Contras's place? He fervently hoped not, but he had to be sure. Looking around in the darkness, he took a chance and moved out of the shadows.

Maybe the horses had not wandered off too far. In the shadowy brush, he slipped through the mesquite. With care, he checked the outline of his house. Surely the snipers had left, or they would have taken another shot at him by this time.

He located the ground-tied bay. Speaking softly, he was able to walk up to him. Archie must have bolted off. Checking the cinch first, Jed mounted and gave a lost look towards the homestead.

Brackeen, he vowed, *you have just declared war!*

It wasn't enough that the big rancher had tried to crowd the range. He'd hired back-shooters and tried to get Jed arrested. Well, the old bastard had gone too far this time.

He jerked the gelding around, mounted, and set spurs to him. If Brackeen's men had harmed a hair on Gabriella's head, they'd not only answer to that old Mexican bandit, they'd answer to him, too.

CHAPTER No. 9

Neemore sat in his parlor trying to read a law book, but he couldn't concentrate. He was still upset and angry about the shooting incident in the courthouse yard. All afternoon he had been considering a long list of county residents better suited than Blythe to be a deputy.

"Neemore Davis, you have not heard one word I've said all evening," Josie complained.

He closed the book and looked at his wife.

"What is wrong with you?"

Neemore grunted. "Lord Almighty, Josie! I nearly got killed today because of that stupid Blythe, and yet you expect me to sit around and chit-chat with you like some damned social talker."

"*See?*" She pounced on his word. "There you go getting angry again."

"Well?"

"Well, I didn't shoot at you, and it seems

to me you could try and discuss the matter with your wife in a civilized manner."

"Josie, I'm sorry, but I have a lot on my mind."

She picked up the embroidery hoop in her lap. "Well, if you don't want to talk about it."

"Ah, Josie." Neemore shook his head ruefully. "It's hard being a good commissioner in a place as uncivilized as this . . . take that old ex-ranger, Alex, for instance. He ain't got good sense, shooting two strangers like he did. Now mind you, they probably needed killing, but why not leave it to someone else. If word gets out, folks will think we're plumb gun happy."

Josie clucked her tongue in sympathy. "I can understand your concern. Alex should have realized how important a good reputation is for a man of your stature and position."

"Exactly. Then there's that dumb stunt that Blythe pulled today." His brows drew together every time he recalled the deputy's foolish act.

"Neemore." Her voice had turned soft, almost provocative. "There is a good breeze tonight. Perhaps you would share my room with me?"

Neemore blinked, his mouth opened in

surprise. Was Josie asking him to go to bed with her? She hadn't done that in years. Hell — it had been nearly *five* years. He smiled and stood abruptly. "I'll lock up the house and be right up."

He watched the spry swish of her brown skirt as she climbed the stairs. Actually, it had not been five years since he had been to bed with his wife, he admitted honestly. But it had been that long since she had *invited* him to share her bed.

Turning, he hurried to the kitchen and turned the key that always hung in the door keyhole. Then he blew out the lamp and climbed the stairs.

Only starlight and a pale moon shone through the windows. Josie must have already gotten into bed. As he undressed in the dark, he wondered what she was wearing. Damn, it would probably be something with ninety buttons on it, clear to her ankles. Why the hell couldn't she for once go to bed bare-ass naked like Dolores did all the time?

From the bedroom door, her breathing sounded a little excited. He smiled in anticipation as he struggled out of his one-piece underwear.

"Josie?"

"Yes, Neemore?" she whispered breathlessly.

"I've been thinking. We need to go to San Antone or Ft. Worth for a week or so. We could stay at a nice hotel and see how civilized folks live."

"That would be very nice. I'd really enjoy that. You are such a good husband, Neemore."

He felt a momentary twinge of guilt, which he quickly stifled. Moving through the darkness, he searched for the right side of the bed. Slipping under the flannel sheet, he closed his eyes in irritation. The damned sheet was hot as an Angora rug. When he placed his hand on her chest, he choked back a groan. How in the hell she managed to climb into the long, button-up gown in the little time it had taken him to lock the doors, he'd never know.

"Neemore," she said quietly, her hands lying limply by her sides, "do you still feel the same way about me as you did when we first married?"

"Sure." His fingers fumbled down the row of buttons on her gown. He kissed her cheek and finally pushed the gown open. The feel of her skin, which was still soft, made his blood race. He rose to his knees and moved across her, until he was between her thighs.

Then the sound of horse hooves pounded to an abrupt halt just below the window and someone shouted his name.

Josie panicked and bolted upright beneath him, nearly knocking him over. "My gawd, Neemore, they'll know what we're doing!"

"Aw, shit!" Neemore scowled. He climbed off the bed and crossed to the window, pushed back the curtain, and stuck his head outside. "What is it?"

"Judge, we've got trouble!" Mike Wells shouted up at him. "Jed Mahan shot Shoat Smith tonight."

"What the hell for?" He jerked his arm away from his wife who was trying to pull him back inside.

"You're plumb *naked*!"

"He can't see nothing but my chest. Go back to bed, Josie." Neemore turned back to the window and dimly made out Wells's form on the horse.

"Where in hell is Alex?"

"Gone to arrest Mahan."

"Why do you reckon Jed shot the boy?"

"Got into a ruckus over cards, I guess. Two of Brackeen's men saw him ride off from where they found Shoat's body."

"All right. I'll be down after I get dressed."

His brows pleated together, and he ran a hand over his bald pate in puzzlement.

Something was wrong with Wells's story. It just didn't make sense. That Smith boy had ridden into town with Mahan less than five hours ago.

Jed Mahan was cocky at times, but it didn't seem likely that he would cold-bloodedly shoot the boy. No, Neemore decided as he pulled on his clothes, it just didn't add up.

Jed rode through the darkened Texas range, his jaw clenched in anger. His eyes narrowed as his imagination conjured up a violent picture. If those bushwhackers had attacked Gabriella trying to get to him, they'd be sorry. He spurred the bay on, vowing to find the ambushers and make them pay heavily if Gabriella was harmed in any way.

The thought of Brackeen's unchecked power raised his ire. It was time someone put ol' Charlie in his place, he fumed.

And that place just might be under a tombstone.

Tree limbs tore at Jed as he galloped toward Gabriella's, but the stinging branches only fired his anger. He stopped on the edge of the canyon above Gabriella's house. The dogs were barking.

The sound filled him with relief. If the

dogs were all right, that meant that Gabriella was safe. Sighing thankfully, Jed headed the horse down the steep slope.

A light came on inside the house. No doubt the barking dogs had awakened Gabriella. When he was in the yard, Jed shouted, "Hold your fire, Gabby! It's me — Jed!"

She stood in the doorway, her duster wrapped around her and a shotgun in her hands. The light fell behind her so that her face was in the shadow.

"So, you came back." Her tone was less than welcoming.

"Has anyone been here?"

"No." She placed the gun back inside against the door. "Did you expect someone to?"

He sighed heavily. No doubt she was still in an angry mood, but he was too tired to play games. "Listen. Two men were waiting for me when I got home. They shot at me. I rode the hell out of my horse, 'cause I was worried they might come here. Gabriella, I'm tired, and I don't feel like having a repeat of this afternoon."

"But why would they shoot at you?"

He ran his hand around the back of his neck. He felt so weary his legs cramped and felt as heavy as bars of lead. "I guess Char-

135

lie figures I'm a threat or something. Or maybe those two deputies are still after me. Hell, I don't know. Seems I got more enemies than dogs got fleas. If you're all right, then I guess I'll just ride on back home."

"Come, Jed, you are tired." Her voice softened, and she put her hand on his arm to pull him inside. "Come to bed."

Numbly, Jed walked beside her, only vaguely aware of her helping him undress. Before she blew out the lantern, the bed engulfed his weary body, and he fell into a deep sleep filled with dreams and memories alike.

The lariat around his chest pinned his arms to his side. He had been riding his short-coupled pony after some yearlings. He'd not even heard the swish of the rope, but his bones were jarred when he was jerked from his saddle. Knocked breathless, he cringed from the ominously powerful horse legs surrounding him. When he dared look up, Charles Brackeen's cold, gray eyes seemed to bore a hole in him. "Boy, when you chase those stringy Mexican steers of yours, be sure you don't run the fat off any B-Bar-M cattle."

Dumbstruck, he stared wide-eyed at the chiseled face and grim set of Brackeen's rigid jaw. He could feel the power and authority radiating down from the biggest rancher in Callie County.

"Boss you want me to drag him through a little prickly pear?" the gravelly voiced belonged to the B-Bar-M foreman, Buster Deets.

"Boy, don't you know better than to chase B-Bar-M cattle?" Charlie demanded.

Too frightened to raise his hands and push the rope, he mumbled, "Yes, sir." Still worried, he watched the rancher turn to the grinning foreman. Brackeen appeared impatient with Deets's idea of punishment.

"Get the rope off him, Buster!"

Jed sat on the ground and watched the rancher and his men ride away. Deets looked over his shoulder and grinned, his hands busy coiling his rope as he rode.

Jed jerked awake, bathed in sweat.

The room was in total darkness. For a moment, he couldn't remember where he was. His heart hammered as though he had just run a race. When he heard Gabriella's soft breathing beside him, he blew out a deep sigh.

Lying back down, Jed stared thoughtfully in the darkness. Charlie Brackeen had been his enemy since before his father died years ago. Jed remembered the day they laid William Mahan to rest beside his wife. It had been just a few days before Jed's nineteenth birthday. Despite the doctor's medicines and housecalls, the life had drained out of Bill Mahan, inch by painful inch. It seemed his will to live had just dried up like the parched land they had ranched.

He recalled his father's reaction on the day of the lariat incident. He had been unsympathetic and issued his own warning. His leathered face held little patience. "Well, stay out of that rich sumbitch's way. He's tough, and besides, the man has a point. Cattlemen don't like the fat run off their cattle."

After he got over the initial humiliation, Jed had accepted his father's words. His advice had worked . . . up until now. Now, suddenly, Charlie Brackeen wanted more. He was an old man, and maybe he had begun to believe he really was the king of Callie County.

Thumping the bed with his fist, Jed gritted his teeth. There had to be a way to stop him from taking over the small ranchers' ranges. Maybe if Brackeen suffered some severe cattle losses, he'd see he was no longer king.

A soft hand fell on his bare thigh. He tensed, then relaxed and smiled in the darkness. A quiet sigh escaped him, and he reached for Gabriella.

The dogs began to bark viciously outside.

"Who is that?" She half-rose, then swung out of bed. After pulling on a robe, she moved toward the kitchen.

"Be careful." He hurriedly climbed out of bed and pulled on his pants. Then he strapped on his pistol, his ears picking up the sound of horse's hooves.

In the kitchen, he kept back, staying in the shadows out of sight. He watched Gabriella pick up the rifle and open the door.

"Hold your fire, Mrs. Contras!" The sheriff's gruff voice came sharply on the night air. "I need Jed Mahan. Tell him to give himself up. He's wanted for the murder of Shoat Smith."

Jed sucked a breath. What the hell?

The sheriff continued. "Tell him to give himself up now or a lynch mob will get him."

Gabriella cocked the Winchester. "Stay on your horse."

He was stunned by the news of Shoat's death. If someone killed Shoat Smith, it had to be one of Brackeen's back shooters or one of Alex's flunkies. How in the *hell* were they planning to pin the murder on *him*?

Poor Shoat had wanted a fight, but he'd probably been shot in the back.

His hands clenched, Jed swore. He'd been

set up. Framed. What the hell was he going to do about it? It was almost a certainty Woodbridge had not come out there alone to get him. He probably had his deputies along, backing him up.

He tried to quell his anger and consider his options.

The sheriff was tougher than both deputies put together, by a long damn way. Though he might escape, Jed knew the chances were better that he'd be shot. The only question left was whether he would survive the ride to town, or be back-shot on the way 'resisting arrest.'

Well, shit. With odds like those. . . .

His decision made, Jed stepped into the kitchen doorway. "Woodbridge! Hold your fire!"

Gabriella gaped at him. "What is *wrong* with you?"

"I'll handle this. I'll strike a deal with the sheriff." He had raised his voice on the last words.

Woodbridge heard him. "How's that?"

"First, we both know I never shot Shoat Smith. Let's get that straight. Secondly, me and Gabriella could just as easily shoot you and those deputies out there with you. So, I figure if y'all will ride on back to No Gap, then I'll follow you the day after tomorrow.

We can settle this then. A day or so ain't going to make any difference." He kept behind the adobe wall inside the door as he waited for a response.

His Colt was ready. The sharp tang of burnt powder from the barrel stung his nostrils.

The sheriff's laconic voice drifted back in through the open door. "Ain't no need in getting that woman shot up. Don't you take no notion of jingle-bobbing off out of the country, Jed." The words were a warning he clearly understood. He knew the bandy-legged sheriff would set in on a track if he left out.

"Deal! Only tell them two dumbass deputies how it works, too. Maybe draw them a picture."

"They'll know how it is. You just be in No Gap by that sundown day after tomorrow."

Gabriella stepped inside next to him. "Do you trust him?"

He slowly shook his head. "I'm not sure."

"Well, Alex is better than the other two. They are stupid. But the sheriff is like Pablo — an old tiger, yes?"

A brief smile curved his lips. "Sounds like they're leaving, but I don't trust them. I figure the deputies got the south trail covered. The old tiger'll cover the road leading to No Gap."

"You don't believe them?"

"No. Woodbridge don't give up that easy. Somebody else shot Shoat. If I get killed running away, they can close the case. That'll let the real killers off the hook."

Gabriella had lit the lamp in the kitchen. She had her head cocked, listening to the sounds outside. There was no barking from her dogs. With a look of satisfaction, she loaded her wood stove with kindling.

Jed sat down heavily in the high-back wooden chair. His fingers drummed the table. "I figure if they can get Neal Smith to believe I shot his son, it will split up the ranchers who are on my side. Divided, there'll be no defense to stand against Brackeen."

"*You* figured all that out?" She looked at him with raised eyebrows. "All by yourself?"

Jed grinned at her sarcasm. "I know Brackeen. It's the way he would think."

"So, what will you do?"

He closed his eyes and rubbed his face. "I'm not sure, but I only have about a day to do it in."

Gabriella nodded.

His fingers drummed on the table, his mind racing over and rejecting plan after plan.

CHAPTER NO. 10

On Thursday morning, Neemore ate his cold grits and tried to imagine a just revenge on the whole population of Callie County. First, he would slowly torture that damned deputy — Wells — who interrupted his marital relations with Josie. The fact that he'd waited *months* for such an opportunity and then had been foiled at the last minute filled him with rage. Wells's untimely interruption had been a boot-kicking aggravation that made his teeth ache from clenching them so tight.

And after he finished with Wells, Neemore schemed he'd torture that gun-happy idiot Blythe. It was too bad Jed Mahan's committee had all missed him. Instead of Blythe, their barrage of bullets had destroyed the courthouse windows and scattered grit over his own prone body. As if there weren't enough problems in Callie County, now someone was accusing Jed of killing Shoat

Smith. The death of the oldest son of the Tennessee farmer was no great loss to the county to be sure, but having Jed Mahan accused of the crime was a different matter.

Neemore paused in his observations when Rosalina brought his coffee.

"The windmill is fixed," she said with a smug smile.

Neemore scowled at the irritating sound of her scuffling feet. Did she expect praise because her husband had done the job he'd been hired for? Since he didn't want to get into a quarrel with the contrary woman, he ignored her. He had enough on his mind without bickering with his damned fat-assed housekeeper.

He finished his meal in silence. There was no doubt he'd have to ride out to Charlie Brackeen's place. The cattle drive Charlie had planned would only stir up more ranchers. And Jed Mahan sitting in jail out of his way wasn't going to make a hell of a lot of difference. The ranchers would simply pick a new leader.

It might take a little time, but Neemore was sure they weren't going to give in easily to Charlie's invasion of their territory. The smaller outfits would be ready when he began pushing his cattle across Dead Horse Creek. A range war was as inevitable as

Alex's shooting of the two drifters in the saloon. It was just a matter of time.

Wiping his mouth on his napkin, he stood. There were a lot of things he had to do today.

First, he would go see about getting the glass replaced in the courthouse windows. The empty frames wouldn't make a favorable impression if some official from Austin came snooping around. Neemore surmised that the glass would have to come all the way from San Antone, and that would take some time.

The judge glanced up the stairs toward Josie's room. He shook his head regretfully, then unlocked the front door. Teeth clenched, he went outside into the cool morning air. When he stepped inside Alex's office a few minutes later, his mood was not improved any by the sight of the town sheriff.

Alex was slumped in his chair. He opened his one good eye but didn't bother to sit up.

"Well? Did you get Mahan?"

"The boys will bring him in." He slid lower in his chair and pushed his hat forward.

Neemore's anger rose at the indifferent attitude. "I thought *you* were going to bring him in."

145

A harsh sigh escaped Alex's lips as he sat up and pushed his hat back. His cold blue eye fixed upon Neemore with blazing intensity. "Hell, I'm the sheriff. I said we'll bring him in, and we will. There wasn't any sense in shooting up Contras's place. Mahan will stir out eventually, and my men will grab him."

"They couldn't grab their own *asses!*"

"What's got you all riled up?" Woodbridge frowned, his thin silver brows drawing together.

With difficulty, Neemore swallowed back his anger. "I think it's about time we either straighten out this damned mess, or —" He stopped in mid-sentence, not sure how to finish his statement.

Alex shook his head. "You're just all worked up. Hell, in two weeks this'll all blow over. We've been through worse things before."

A chatter of voices outside prevented Neemore from answering, a spate of excited Spanish. The woman who burst into Woodbridge's office was Juan Gonzales's wife.

"Sheriff! That no good son of a *puta,* he steals my goat." She pointed behind her, the action exposing the rounded tops of her ample breasts. "You must do something!"

Neemore wondered idly if the goat rustler

in question had followed the woman and children into the courthouse. "Who stole your goat?"

"That no good Flores!"

Neemore tried to recall the old man Lupe referred to. Flores was a woodcutter by trade, and he doubted whether the slow moving, gray-haired Mexican could capture a goat unless he caught it while it slept.

Alex sighed in frustration. "What did he do with it?"

"Listen! He. Stole. My. *Goat.*" Lupe Gonzalez turned and gestured wildly with her brown hands as she translated for her companions.

The sheriff stood, his face carved in lines of anger. "Well, go get it back from him. Hell, surely you can take your own goat back home."

Neemore studied the woman's flushed face. She was about to explode. "How can I bring him home when that old *bastardo* ate him?"

"Are you sure it was your goat?"

"Am I sure?" She screeched, jumping up and down. "Of course, it is my goat. Am I stupid? Why did I come here?" She lapsed into a string of Spanish that sounded like prayers mixed with curses. Shifting restlessly, Neemore couldn't help but notice in her agitation, her breasts were heaving.

"Now wait a damned minute!" Alex waved everyone back into the hall. "When my deputy comes in, we'll go arrest Flores and find out if he ate your goat."

"He *did*!"

"I know, I know. But, Mrs. Gonzalez, I'm covered up right now. I'll send Blythe over there, and he can figure all this out."

"Ha! Your deputy will be no help. He is too *stupid*." She scoffed and spat on the floor. "And damned old Flores will eat *all* my goats."

"Well, who the hell gives a —"

"We'll settle this." Neemore interrupted before Alex lost all composure. "You see, Mrs. Gonzalez, a boy was murdered yesterday. As soon as we get his killer rounded up, we'll question *Señor* Flores."

"I cannot help this murder. Flores killed my fattest goat!"

Neemore put a hand beneath her elbow and ushered her outside the office, offering soothing platitudes. Thankfully, the woman and her rowdy support group were temporarily appeased by this. They crossed the courtyard chattering as they headed for home.

He went back inside the sheriff's office. Alex was pacing. The lines of his craggy face were deeper than ever. He gave the judge a look of resignation.

"I'll send Blythe over to look into the matter."

Neemore raised his brows. "Maybe he can do something that simple, but if I were you, I'd go along personally. If he's left alone, he might end up shooting all her goats."

"Blythe ain't that bad."

"No?" He sighed. "Well, between the two of you, I've nearly been killed twice in as many days. Tell me, is there some kind of conspiracy to murder the Callie County Judge and Commissioner? To hell with it all. I'm going to see if I can get Swafford to order me some new window glass."

He didn't wait for any comment from Alex. He stomped outside and crossed the courtyard.

A rig was parked over at the undertaker's — probably the Smiths. God, he hoped that the Smiths would not request him to speak at the boy's funeral. There was a preacher who would come around if the priest down at the mission didn't show up to say a Hail Mary. Neemore knew the Protestant by sight, but his name eluded him now. But with the temperature rising steadily, the Smiths would have to bury the boy quickly.

Neemore entered Swafford's store, and

the smell of dry goods and spices assailed his nose.

The tall middle-aged store owner beamed a welcoming smile. Swafford seemed amused about the previous day's shooting incident. "Things quieter today, Judge Davis?"

"I just spoke to the sheriff about that matter. Tom, I need those two windows in the courthouse replaced." Neemore took out his gold watch and glanced at it. "And I think you better send someone to San Antone who has enough sense to get it back here in one piece."

"I think I can get someone to, but it'll cost you some."

"How much?"

The storekeeper pinched his chin and frowned thoughtfully. "You mean all together?"

"Of *course,* all together."

"Well, reckon it'll come close to twenty dollars."

The judge exhaled a deep breath. "For a dollar, I'd board them up, but we have to keep up our image. Callie County is a progressive place. I'd hate for the governor to come by and see the east side of our courthouse all boarded up. Send your man after the glass. And, Tom?"

"Yes, sir, Judge?"

Neemore selected some black cigars before he finished his sentence. "Tell the son of a bitch to get them here in one piece." He waved the cigars. "Put these on my bill."

"Sure will." Tom paused. "And we'll get them here in one piece. Don't you worry."

Neemore glanced at his watch again, then snapped it shut. "Thanks. I knew you could handle it." The judge walked out into the bright sunshine. His steps slowed as he headed back to his office, the dread of returning weighing heavily upon him. Some days, it just wasn't worth the effort of getting out of bed.

Well, if nothing else, at least he could smoke a good cigar to help pass away the time as he worried.

Jed Mahan considered a plan to escape the obvious trap Alex Woodbridge had set for him. In all probability, he'd left the deputies behind on both routes leading from No Gap to Gabriella's place. If he managed to escape, the two deputies would still be on his trail.

He pushed his empty plate across the table and spoke musingly to Gabriella. "I think I've got an idea."

She scraped out a plate and nodded. He

looked at her profile. She seemed pale today. Perhaps she'd already lost the baby, but he wasn't going to ask her.

Scowling, he dismissed the tasteless subject from his mind. "This idea of mine is to shoot off our guns, and when the deputies come in, I'll cover them, then tie you three up."

"Three?" She gave him a look that said his plan had failed to impress her.

"Yah, otherwise they can arrest you for helping me."

"Bad idea." She resumed washing the dishes. "Wait until dark and ride by them. You can do that."

He shook his head. "No, that'll be too late. I want to get out and find out who shot Shoat."

"That is easy. Find out who said you did it. How else do they know you shot him, when you didn't?"

Her logic was unassailable. He laughed. "Great reasoning. Only I don't know who said I shot him."

"*Sí.* But you can bet one thing, Jed." He waited for her to continue. "Brackeen! He is behind all this."

She was right, of course. "Can I lead a horse up this canyon and get out to the west?"

"Sure. If you are a goat."

He took out his tobacco and rolled a cigarette. The steep draw behind her place seemed to be the only way out. Since the dogs weren't barking, the deputies were obviously stationed at a discreet distance from the homestead. Woodbridge was smart enough to know the dogs would be restless if they scented the deputies. If he slipped west, he might get by without either of them seeing him. Then he could ride to the Allen's place and find out who'd said he shot Shoat.

"I'm going to saddle my horse. You keep the dogs quiet. If they go to raising cane, those deputies are liable to move in."

Gabriella nodded and wiped her hands. "You be careful."

"I will. Just keep those curs quiet." He pushed out of the chair. Gabriella went to the back door and began calling softly to the dogs. Obediently, one-by-one they gathered around her. Jed grinned, then went out to the corral where Gabriella had put his bay. Quickly saddling the gelding, he kept a watchful eye on the canyon walls half-hidden by the mesquite and live oak trees.

He bounded into the saddle. "I'll be back."

"You must always come back to Gabriella, yes?"

"Always." Jed lifted the reins, then stopped as a thought occurred to him. "Hey . . . did you mean what you said when I rode off yesterday? About loving me?"

His Mexican beauty grinned coyly. Standing on her tiptoes, she leaned into the horse and beckoned him closer with the wag of her finger. When he leaned down, she kissed him once quickly on the lips. "To find out, you must come back to me."

"Thanks, Gabby." He lifted the reins and headed westward. Her goats scattered before him, bleating in protest. She hadn't been lying. The trail up the sidewall was only a goat track. The sheer face forced Jed to dismount, and even the bay found the footing treacherous. Slowly but surely, they climbed together, not daring to look down.

They were both bathed in sweat when they reached the top. When Jed finally looked back, he was amazed that he had been able to get them up the canyon. Stepping in the stirrups, he swung in the saddle and headed south. He glanced at the high sun. If he avoided the roads and Woodbridge's deputies, the ride to Allen's ranch would take several hours. Hours of hot, watchful riding for him.

Jed reached the Allen's place late in the afternoon. Et Allen came out on the porch and shouted down her dogs. "Good grief, Jed Mahan, what are you into now?"

He dismounted and hitched the gelding to the yard fence. "Where's Sam?"

"Gone to see if he can help Neal. Guess you know Shoat got hisself killed up at the Springs?"

With a grim nod, Jed looked about the yard as he walked towards the porch. "They're accusing me of it."

"Yeah, I heard. It figures." She shook her gray head. "Come on in. Sam said they were wrong about you. I'll bet Neal don't believe it, either."

He followed her inside. "Who found the body?"

"A couple of B-Bar-M hands, I reckon. Said they found him over north of Dead Horse Creek." She moved to the stove and came across to pour him a cup of black coffee. "Mrs. Oliver came by here this morning. That danged old busybody knew all about it. Sam saddled up and went to see if he could help Neal. I would've gone, too, but with his wife being pure Indian, I figured I wouldn't be able to comfort her. You know what I mean?"

He nodded and studied the steaming cof-

155

fee. Cursing soundlessly, he grew rigid as a vision of the powerful rancher burned before his eyes.

Damn you, Charlie! This time you'll pay, or I'll go down fighting.

"You all right, Jed?"

"Ah, I'm just worried." It was only partly a lie. The emotions clouding his mind seemed more vengeful than angry. "Brackeen is behind all this, Et. And I'm ready to call him out and settle this once and for all, whether it's win, lose, or draw."

"Oh, Jed, don't be foolish. Wait till Sam gets back. He'll have a better plan. You can't go barging in on Brackeen. Why, he'd cut you to ribbons."

Giving her a determined look, Jed remained silent.

"Do you want something to eat?"

He shook his head and stared at the wall. "No time. I have to find a way to prove that I didn't shoot Shoat. Damn, I nearly went up there last night to check on him. Instead, I went home and was welcomed by two of Brackeen's back-shooters."

She refilled his cup. "You have any idea who they were?"

"No, but I will shortly. Tell Sam I may need lots of help, but for now, I have something in mind."

Returning the granite pot to the stove, she slammed it down and spoke dryly, "And just what might that be?"

"I'm going to catch me a Brackeen hand and get the truth out of him."

"They're sure to be on guard against something like that."

Jed's mouth set obstinately. His eyes narrowed into slits as anger swelled inside him. "By damned, Et, they must have shot the boy."

He stood abruptly and swallowed the coffee. After wiping his mouth on his sleeve, he nodded thanks to the rancher's wife and moved toward the door.

CHAPTER NO. 11

Neemore Davis was in a quandary. If he went down to Ben's Trace and spent a couple hours with Dolores, he would have to sleep on the back porch again. There would be no sharing his attention with two women in one day.

A trickle of sweat ran beneath his starched white shirt. Sometimes putting in his time as a public official was hell. At the moment, he was still having difficulty accepting the possibility that Jed Mahan had shot the Smith boy. After giving the matter a great deal of consideration, he came to the conclusion that if Jed had actually shot Shoat, it was because they were drunk. That was the only plausible explanation. Guns were poor decisionmakers, especially when liquor was involved.

Thinking about making decisions reminded Neemore of Alex's increasingly bad attitude. Leaving his deputies out at the

Contras's place was not a good idea. Alex should have stayed with them.

He wiped his face with a white linen handkerchief. He decided he *would* go see Dolores later. The chances of Josie wanting to do something two nights in a row were damned slim. Besides, there was nothing else to do right now. Other than that fat, farting woodcutter Flores eating the wrong goat again, it was unlikely that the services of the judge would be needed on a hot Thursday afternoon in No Gap.

Hell, that case wouldn't be worth dusting out the courtroom for. It would be a circus with that voluptuous Lupe Gonzales waving her brown arms and screaming in Spanish with all her kinfolk joining in. Old Flores would be sitting on the witness chair, his beady black eyes as mean as a fighting rooster's. His relatives would be on the other side screaming that the Lopez family didn't eat goats — they bred them. Not believing another such storm would fall in his lap, he shook his head to dissolve the picture. That kind of trial did not fulfill his expectations of courtroom procedures.

Placing his hands flat on the desktop, he pushed himself up and crossed the hall to find Alex asleep under his *sombrero.* Flies buzzed around his clasped hands which lay

159

across his chest. His fingers jerked involuntarily flicking away the insects.

"Alex, I'll be back."

"Uh-huh." The sheriff nodded, but didn't bother to raise his head.

Casting an irritated frown at the lawman, Neemore sighed heavily and turned toward the door. Surely, Woodbridge was capable of handling the place for a while — even if it was unusual for the old buzzard to sleep during the daytime.

Maybe he was feeling his age.

As he passed the undertaker's front door, he shook his head. He knew the Smith boy had been buried. He'd watched the funeral wagon go by, and later saw Sloan drive it back and park it. A quiet crowd of "southend" people had followed the wagon. Their silence had been eerie.

It unnerved him, making him feel guilty because no county officials had been present at the funeral. Alex hadn't bothered to go, and somehow Neemore hadn't felt he would be welcome.

He'd paid his respects to the family, including the boy's mother. Neemore couldn't ever remember seeing the Indian woman in town before. When he stopped by the undertaker's to offer his sympathy to Neal Smith, he'd felt uneasy. And it had

160

been odd that there was no talk of a hanging, no mention of Jed Mahan's. The whole situation was damn peculiar.

When he passed by Ben's Saloon, he noticed several B-Bar-M hands among the crowd inside, getting liquored up before going down to the Trace. It was unusual for the hands to be in town on a weekday, but Neemore supposed that since the weather was so dry, and roundup over, Charlie had given them some time off. Still, he felt uncomfortable about their presence. Something told him those boys were in No Gap for a reason.

Neemore shook his head, not wanting to even speculate what that reason might be.

Moving slow in the growing heat, he passed by the outhouse, holding his breath against the offensive odor. He stopped on the shaded footpath leading to the brown tents.

The rows of tents reminded him of the Army tents he'd spent many nights in. He'd slept on a cot and listened to guns roaring like summer thunder in the distance. Working as an adjutant to General Hap Thornton, Neemore had spent more time keeping books than shooting. Someone had to keep the books, after all. Besides, it had been a bloody war that he didn't mind missing.

161

There had been a shortage of everything, even shoes. Hell, men had worn the soles of their feet to the bone. The only clothes available were those stolen from dead soldiers. And there had been plenty of dead to steal from. He'd gotten to the point where he hated anything gray. Even the fleas chewing on him had been the sickly gray color. Men had come into camp so hollow-eyed, they appeared to be mere wraiths. Dragging their rifles by the barrel, they were beyond hunger and nearer starvation. He shook his head to banish the ugly scenes.

Gratefully, he reached Dolores's tent and raised the canvas flap. "Dolores? Have you got time for me today?"

"Come in, *Señor.*" She smiled, and a warm glow spread across her brown face. In an instant, she rose from the packing crate and hurried to pull down the tent flaps behind him.

"Where have you been?"

"You wouldn't believe it." He began while taking off his vest. She deftly helped him undress. Her almond-shaped brown eyes danced with pleasure.

"It's been a long time."

"*Sí.*" Laughing, she pulled off his boots. He enjoyed the attention. This little Mexican gal was a professional and knew how to make a man relax. And that was just what he needed, at the moment, to take his mind off his frustrating problems. He smiled and leaned back on the cot.

Jed rode the bay northward from the Allen's place. Et had filled a bag with some jerky, coffee beans, and cold biscuits. The poke hung on his saddlehorn and swung gently as the horse trotted toward the country where Shoat had been shot.

Careful to avoid the main roads, Jed chose cow trails and game paths, instead. He kept the .45 Colt on his hip, feeling for it often. With his knowledge of the range country, he moved across the area quickly without human contact. At sundown, he reached Dead Horse Creek.

Under the tall cypress trees, he kept a watchful eye on the shallow ford, although he knew it was seldom used. He let the gelding drink his fill before crossing the creek. The shadows of the growing darkness were deeper. Night insects began a raspy serenade, and bats swooped after them in silent flight. From a ridge, he looked for signs of a campfire. If Charlie had left a guard on duty, there would be a fire.

Jed kept to the high country but didn't detect wood smoke, nor did he see any lights in the brush. He wondered if there was anyone in the country looking after this sound "dead line" of Brackeen's.

If there were any cowboys stationed out here, he hadn't found any indications of their position. Later, Jed dismounted to relieve himself. So far, his plan to capture one of Brackeen's men was not working. Here in the vast brush country there seemed to be only him and the mournful coyotes howling at the slowly rising moon. His surveillance completed, he remounted and took a star-lit path off the escarpment. The gelding was sure-footed, and he had faith in the horse's ability to pick a safe route in the night.

The big dipper appeared to point out the trail, and he wearily followed it. When a night hawk sprung off a nearby stump, it sent his hand flying to his holster. Realizing that it had only been a bird, he settled back in the saddle, smiling in chagrin. He really *was* edgy. But he was so far into the enemy camp, it paid to be cautious. It was a fool's mission to go to the B-Bar-M without backup, and he knew he would only have himself to blame if he got caught. There would be no quarter given where he was going. By this time, it would be open season on him, him being a wanted murderer and all. Charlie Brackeen might just be savoring that fact like the aroma of strips of bacon in a sizzling skillet.

Despite his precarious position, the comparison made Jed's mouth water. He took a strip of jerky from the poke and rehung the sack on the saddlehorn. Chewing helped pass the time through the quiet night. He twisted in the saddle and strained his ears.

Nothing.

He sighed, the sound of his own breathing too loud in the darkness.

His mind was bogged down by conflicting emotions and ideas. If he happened to ride upon Charlie, he had no definite plan in mind. Maybe he would push a cocked pistol in Charlie's gut and demand that the big rancher stop harassing him. But he realized that, after extracting a promise worth less than a sun-cured cow pile, he'd be shot as soon as he stepped back and holstered his gun.

No. There had to be a better answer.

Whoever killed Shoat needed to take his place on the hanging scaffold. There were too many problems and no way of solving them. It was a frightening thought. The moon shone at three-quarters across the sky when he dismounted and scouted the outer perimeter of Brackeen's ranch headquarters. His spurs hung on the saddlehorn where he'd hitched the bay.

From this vantage point, he could see an armed guard's silhouette. The man ambled from the corral to the shadowy darkness of a live oak.

God, this was crazy. He was about to take on the whole damn Brackeen camp. He was not sure if his nerves were steel enough for the mission, but it was better than doing nothing.

He crept along the shadows of the corral until he saw the red flicker of a match. A whiff of tobacco smoke caused him to pause abruptly, then the sound of someone sucking at a pipe.

The man was about thirty feet away, with his back to him. It was a good thing Brackeen hated dogs so much. A pack of curs would have set up a holy racket by now. The guard leaned his rifle against a tree and fussed with his pipe. In one lithe movement, Jed moved and drove the barrel of his pistol into the man's back.

"One word, and you meet your maker." Deftly he drew the man's pistol and shoved it into his own waistband. "How many guards?"

He prodded his gun barrel in the man's

back for effect.

"Me. Only me."

Jed wasn't sure if the man was lying or not, but he had to make a quick decision. If the guard was telling the truth, he could afford to take chances that he wouldn't attempt otherwise. With his gun barrel directing the man, he forced him toward a nearby shed. Within a few minutes, he'd tied up the guard and gagged him with the man's own handkerchief. The cowboy undoubtedly expected to be shot, and therefore behaved as a model prisoner at a fate far less than he expected.

"Where's Brackeen?" Jed demanded.

Only a muffled noise came from the guard. He lowered the gag and gave the man a rough shove to enforce his authority.

"Where is he?"

"San Antone — been there a week or so."

"Are you sure?"

"Sure I'm sure. By gawd, I know when he's gone or not. Hell, man —"

"Shut up." Jed raised the gag over his mouth again. If Charlie Brackeen had been gone for a week, then who in hell was in charge?

Then it came to him.

"Buster Deets." Shit. The old foreman was practically a cripple from all the horse wrecks he'd been in. In fact, he remembered, the old coot nowadays seldom rode out to roundups except in a buckboard. Several times, Jed had heard the B-Bar-M hands talking about Buster. His gravelling voice stung like a bullwhip, and his language was just as cutting.

Jed stood in the shed doorway and glanced around at the scattering of buildings. The big, white frame house was Brackeen's headquarters. The windows were all dark.

A couple of low stone buildings stood to the left of the house. He moved along them toward the sounds of snoring. He sniffed the air, identifying the odor of horses and leather. Then he crept onward past the bunkhouse. Yellow lamplight in the next building cast a patch on the ground, and he heard conversation.

He instantly recognized the gruff tone of Buster Deets.

For a moment he went back in time.

The words, *"Want me to drag him through some prickly pear?"* echoed in his ears. Rage seethed within his head, and he shook himself back to the here and now. Cautiously, Jed edged closer and cocked his head. He could faintly make out Deets's words.

". . . but hell's fire, Alex, Brackeen'll be

168

madder than a hornet! I've got to get a bunch of cattle across that creek. We're out of grass, and it ain't even June yet. This was your plan —"

Woodbridge cut Deets off, but Jed couldn't hear the sheriff's softer words. His teeth clenched, Jed's jaw ached with tension as he strained his ears harder. Finally, he heard Alex say, ". . . goddamn Mahan."

"You know how the old man will be?"

"I'll handle Mahan. Don't worry — he's as good as hung. You get your cattle ready."

His first impulse was to take both pistols and fill the men with lead. Determinedly, he reined in his anger. He was the only witness to the conversation, and if he acted out of anger, he'd have two more murders to hang for. There was nothing to do now but get away from the ranch undetected. He could hear Woodbridge preparing to take his leave. If Deets called for the guard, they'd discover he was gone.

Crouched low, Jed ran behind the bunkhouse. He stumbled over some rails and the dull thuds of the posts hitting the ground sounded like thunder. He tensed, waiting, his hand in his gun. Nothing stirred. On the move again, he stopped at the horse corral and opened the gate. A curious horse snorted at him in the darkness, then moved away, several other ponies following.

Jed smiled as the *remuda* hurried out the open gate. The grass-hungry cow ponies would be scattered by sunup. When Jed reached his gelding, he was out of breath. Untying the reins, he tightened the bay's cinch, then set out south.

If Alex Woodbridge aimed to hang him, he'd have to get a damned fast horse. He trotted his mount into the last beams of moonlight. Deets would have something to worry about now. But, next time, he knew it wouldn't be so easy to catch the crew unaware.

There seemed to be a shovelful of problems to sort out. So, Charlie Brackeen had been gone to San Antone for the past couple of weeks. The old boar was probably denned up in some fuzzy hotel. He may have given the order to shoot anyone who stopped his hands from moving the cattle, but he had no way of knowing it would be Shoat Smith. It probably wouldn't matter to the old man anyway. Brackeen wanted everybody out of his way. That was the law of Brackeen, but it was about time that somebody started questioning his damned law.

CHAPTER NO. 12

Neemore Davis left Dolores and walked back to the courthouse. He noticed the leaves on the trees, shriveled from the heat. It was too damn dry.

But, hell, it was always too damn dry. This was Texas.

Back inside his office, he removed his hat and wiped his forehead with a kerchief. A pair of spurs clanged down the hallway. Damn Woodbridge. He was always scarring the hardwood floors with the confounded things he wore strapped to his boots.

Alex entered the judge's chambers. "I'm taking off now. Going to go see if I can find Mahan myself."

"Fine." Neemore made himself comfortable in his chair. He had no intention of riding going along. "The next time you see Charles, find out if he's celebrating the Fourth of July. Josie was wanting to know."

Alex paused on his way out the door. "He

always has a shindig on the Fourth. Damnit, why didn't you marry a Mexican woman?"

"Well, who riled you up? I never said nothing about your wife. By the way, what in hell are all those B-Bar-M hands doing in town in the middle of the week?"

Woodbridge removed his Stetson and scratched his thinning hair. "Damned if I know. They must be caught up on the work."

"If you believe that, Alex, you'll believe in ghosts and bugbears. What's old Buster up to?" Neemore didn't give him a chance to reply. "Hell, the way I figure it, he must be on his deathbed and not able to keep them brush-poppers busy."

"Maybe they were just caught up."

Neemore cocked a brow in doubt, but did not pursue the subject. "Them two deputies still out at Contras's place waiting for Mahan?"

Alex slammed on his hat, black impatience written on his face. "You know damned well they are. Anything else, Your Honor?" His voice was tinged with acid, "I'll go arrest Flores in the morning, and you can decide who ate the stinking goat."

Unmoved by the display of temper, Neemore nodded. "Fine, but you better call in your deputies, 'cause I figure you'll have hell in the courtroom tomorrow with that hearing."

The other man snorted and stumped out of the office. "We'll get Mahan first."

Neemore checked the green safe behind his desk. It was locked. He hadn't opened the combination lock in days, but it didn't hurt to check it, anyway. He straightened up, his back stiff from the pleasure Dolores had given him. After locking the office door, he went out into the last gasp of the day's heat.

The judge climbed the back steps of his house, absently noting that the yard had been raked. It looked as though his hired hand had been busy. The wind was down, so the windmill wasn't moving. All he needed now was for the damned well to go dry. That would just about cap his list of aggravations.

Before entering the house, he called softly, "It's me, Josie."

Her cheerful voice came back to him from the kitchen, "How was your day, Your Honor?"

Neemore shook his head and moved to the chair to put on his slippers. Rising, he padded into the room. "The biscuits sure smell good."

"Neemore Davis, you say that every evening." She raised up from her position at the oven door and smiled.

"If you had eaten as many gummy *tortillas* as I have, you'd thank the Lord every day for a wife who can bake good biscuits."

His wife laughed gaily. "Any problems at the courthouse?"

After all the years they'd been married, Neemore was still surprised at her naiveté. Did she think every day was deadly dull with nothing but nice orderly cases?

He glanced at his watch then snapped it shut. "Lupe Gonzales claimed that old Flores ate her goat. Both of Alex's deputies are sleeping under a mesquite tree, waiting for Jed Mahan to give himself up. And that old Comanche Killer is scuffing up my halls with his Mexican rowels. I think he's losing his grip."

"My, my." She shook her head and tutted softly. "It sounds like the Callie County judge has had a trying day."

"Just part of the job."

After supper, he tried to read one of his law books. Perhaps Josie would soon tire and go to bed — alone. He fervently hoped so.

Someone knocked on the door.

"Who could that be?" Josie peered over her glasses, then put her sewing down. "I'll answer it."

Neemore nodded, pretending to be absorbed in his book. She went to the door. A moment later, he raised his head at her words, "Neemore, there's a man here who needs to see you. He says it's urgent."

Neemore rose and adjusted his glasses. He stepped into the hall and instantly recognized the waiting man — Jesus Mendez, who worked for Sid Rourke.

"What is it, Jesus?"

The man began to speak rapidly. "It is the cowboys. They are crazy drunk. They are shooting up things. The sheriff, he is gone. No one knows where the deputies are. *Señor* Rourke is very worried. He sent me to get you."

Clapping the worried man on the shoulder, Neemore spoke reassuringly. "Fine. You did the right thing. I'll be along. Tell Rourke I'm coming." He saw the man out, then turned to his wife. Her face was full of anxiety, and her white teeth pulled at her lip.

"Oh, Neemore, you can't go down there."

"Now, Josie, this is my county."

She wrung her hands and looked to the ceiling for help. "You're no match for those wild cowboys."

"I used to be a cowboy, too." He smiled

benignly and, with that, he put on his boots. If he had to settle down a couple of rowdy cowboys, a Greener would be the answer. There was one in the sheriff's office.

Thinking about Alex's again absence filled him with anger. He would certainly give that one-eyed bastard an earful in the morning. But first, he had to calm Josie, so he could get down to the saloon and cool off some drunken cowboys.

"Josie, you hold supper. This will only take a few minutes. Be brave now. I'll be back soon."

When he gave her a hug, he hoped she didn't notice any lingering traces of Dolores's lavender scent upon him. He adjusted his glasses and smiled briefly at her. "Got a job to do."

Josie was almost in hysterics when he closed the front door behind him, but he knew she would be all right. Maybe it wouldn't take long to straighten out the problem at the saloon.

In the darkened courthouse, he felt his way with the aid of the moonlight. When he reached the sheriff's office, he unlocked the door and moved to the gun cabinet. After striking a match, he swore silently. The guns were chained inside the case. He shook his head and stopped to listen to the racket outside. The cowboys were shooting again. If he didn't get over there soon, the holes in the ceiling would make a swamp when it rained.

Frustrated by the chain securing the guns, he lit the lamp on Alex's desk. He pulled out a drawer, but couldn't find a key to the padlock on the chain. When more gunshots punctuated the night, he shut his eyes.

"Alex Woodbridge, I'll kill you with my bare hands." He stomped over to his own office, unlocked the door, and hurried to his desk. After drawing out his long-barreled pistol, he slapped the gun with his other hand. More gunshots came from outside.

Neemore's mouth hurt from clenching his jaw. He strode back to Woodbridge's office and shot the lock twice. Smoke filled the room, and his ears rang from the reports of his revolver. He holstered the pistol in his waistband, then jerked the chain out of the trigger guards and broke open the desk drawer, taking two shells to reload the breech. Next, he stuffed his coat pockets with more cartridges before stalking out of the office into the hall.

Outside, he heard catcalls and shouting. The cowboys were getting stinking drunk.

In the shadows of the courtyard, a single cowboy staggered, clicking his empty pistol and screaming. Neemore slipped behind him and used the barrel of his Navy on the man's head. The cowboy fell to his knees. Neemore struck him again, and finally the man fell face-down in the street. The judge jammed his pistol in his belt and, breathing through his nose, stormed over to the saloon. From the sounds thundering from the place, it seemed like pandemonium. Some of the whores were screaming, glasses were being smashed, and the cowboys' voices were loud and bawdy.

Taking a deep breath, Neemore stepped through the batwing doors and leveled the shotgun. "Everyone get their hands up high."

The sounds trailed away to near silence. Neemore waited until his presence with the scattergun registered throughout the room. A few choked-off curses died away, then the room was silent.

Sid Rourke produced a cut-off model from under the bar as the half-dozen drunks moved backwards to the north wall, hands high in the air. A few were too drunk to realize what was going on, and a couple of cowboys had already passed out.

"Mendez!" Neemore shouted for the man who had brought the message to his house. "Get their guns, Jesus, and their knives, and anything else they might have."

He turned back to the cowboys. "One wrong move, and you'll be in hell instead of my jail. Who in the hell gave you permissions to do all this?" He gestured around with his gun.

The two shotguns had a sobering effect on the cowboys. They had nothing to say. Neemore stepped along the bar. His roving eye caught a figure coming through the back door. The man was singing, but his eyes flew open in surprise at the sight of Neemore and his guns. His next move was the stupidest thing he would ever do.

Neemore saw the man's hand flash to his gun butt. In the man's drunken state, he wouldn't be able to hit a bull in the butt, but he couldn't take the chance.

The cowboy's pistol never cleared leather. The right barrel of the Greener belched fire and smoke. The impact of the buckshot thrust the man back out the door he'd just entered.

A scream from the huddle of women chilled Neemore's blood. He checked on Rourke, then he reloaded. "Who was he?"

"Bob Nelson."

"Well, he's dead now or damned near it." Neemore scowled darkly. "Stupid fool was going for his gun."

179

This wasn't his job, the judge railed inwardly. That skinny old coot of a sheriff was off chasing shadows when he should be in town doing the damned job he was paid to do. The stupid-ass deputies were probably lost out in the Texas brush somewhere.

He looked back at Jesus. "You got all their weapons?"

The Mexican nodded.

"*Señor* Judge?" one of the ladies called to Neemore as he turned to leave.

He turned back around. "Yes?"

"That one owes me two dollars." Her brown finger pointed to the cowboy on the end of the line.

"Put two bucks on the table in front of you." He pointed with the barrel of the shotgun. The tall cowboy, who looked no older than twenty, shrugged and put some money on the table.

"Anymore of you owe these lovely ladies any money?" Neemore looking at each man slowly. Obviously, the rest of the men were debt-free except for what they owed Rourke in damages. The proprietor had been silent the whole time. Neemore knew, in a case like this, a man either talked too much or not at all. Rourke was handling it in the latter fashion.

"If you figure up the damages, Sid, I'll see

that they pay you." Neemore turned back to his charges. "Pick up your buddies. Jesus, first, you get the guns from the boys that are passed out."

The Mexican put the men's hardware on the bar. Neemore waved the Greener barrel towards the door.

"You just wait till Charlie hears about this," one brave cowboy said from the throng.

"Yeah," another hand chimed in. "When he gets back from San Antone, there'll be hell to pay."

"So Charlie's gone to San Antone, huh?" Neemore asked softly. "That's interesting. How long's he been gone?"

"Been gone better'n a week, but he'll be back soon."

Neemore digested the information. Strange that Alex never mentioned Charlie was out of town. Come to think of it, if Charlie was out of town, just who in the hell had Alex gone to see at Brackeen's?

Sighing, he temporarily dismissed the puzzle. He shepherded the drunks toward the jail. "Jesus, I need you to guard the jail."

"*Sí, Señor* Davis. Should I bring their guns?"

"No, come on. Rourke can keep them for security. We got another drunk in the yard over there, and we need to get Andy Sloan to go see about Nelson."

"Is the one in the courtyard dead, too?"

Neemore shook his head. "No, he's just out cold."

"Good." The Mexican shook his head. "I don't like the dead ones."

After locking the conscious and unconscious cowboys inside the cells, Neemore left the small Mexican in Alex's chair with the loaded Greener. He walked back to Rourke's, where someone had laid Nelson on two tables pushed together.

Neemore glanced at the dead man's open eyes. They were blank, bloodshot, staring at nothing — yet seeing something no mortal would ever see. The judge pushed down the eyelids. He couldn't stand to see the open vacant eyes.

"Did you send for Sloan?" He searched through the girls, seeking Dolores. She was not among them, her absence conspicuous and made Neemore uneasy. "Where's Dolores?"

A girl named Roberta looked up from her drink and shook her head in ignorance. "I haven't seen her, Your Honor."

"Well, go see where she is."

The girl stood, pulled up her low-cut dress, and swayed slowly out the back door.

The judge considered kicking her in the slats, but instead, he picked up her unfinished glass of whiskey and downed it.

"Here." Rourke offered a bottle from behind the bar. "I'll pour you some."

"No, thanks." Instead he sat down, shaking his head and awaiting Roberta's return. He pulled the Navy pistol out of his waistband and laid it on the table. The barrel had been gouging him in the groin.

"Oh, *Señor* Judge, come quick!" Roberta called from the door. "I think she is very dead!"

Neemore jerked up from the chair. He looked from her to Rourke, then back to the girl. *"What?"*

"Come, come quickly."

He hurried after the girl. Outside, they followed the moonlit footpath toward the row of tents.

"Is she sure enough dead?" He couldn't believe it was true. Only a few hours ago he had kissed Dolores on her smooth forehead. Who would do such a thing? Dolores had no enemies. He shook his head. No, he couldn't believe she was dead. Perhaps the girl was mistaken.

He nearly collided with Roberta when she came to an abrupt halt outside Dolores's tent.

A small candle lamp flickered inside the tent. The judge ducked inside. Dolores lay sprawled on the cot, her face purple, eyes blank. She appeared to have been choked to death. A shudder of pain shook his entire body. Who the hell had done this? He whispered as if she could hear him, "My gawd, Dolores, who did this to you?"

Her bare breasts shown like small brown mountains, her firm stomach glistened, and her short legs were close together. Her expression was bland.

Dolores was dead.

"Come in here and help me."

"No!" Hysterical, Roberta shook her head and flapped her arms. "No, not with the dead."

"Gawdndamnit! I want her dressed in something. We need to get a priest, and he can't see her naked. Get in here now!"

"Oh!" Roberta gasped in fear as she crept inside.

"Get a hold of yourself, girl."

He chose a black dress from the meager wardrobe and handed it to the fearful Roberta. With effort, he pulled Dolores's limp body into a sitting position. He gave Roberta a black scowl. The girl reluctantly stumbled forward. Dolores's head rolled from side to side as they struggled to dress her. Neemore drew out his kerchief and mopped his brow. His entire body was wet with sweat. Standing motionlessly, he watched Roberta button the dress in the back.

The judge gently rolled his dead lover over, then closed her eyes. He scooped her up in his arms.

"Blow out the light." Roberta quickly leaned over and extinguished the flame with her panting breath. As Neemore carried his precious burden toward Ben's, Dolores's head fell back grotesquely, her long black hair trailing over his arm.

It was a long walk to Ben's Saloon. The full moon filtered through the trees overhead. Neemore didn't dare look down at his burden. He was already sick at the emptiness inside him that her death had brought.

A feeling of impending disaster hung in the hot night air. It wasn't just Dolores's death or the shootout with Nelson, he argued with himself. It was something more. He felt a sense of dread for the future. Even the thought of what tomorrow might bring caused his legs to shake.

Briefly, he closed his eyes, then opened them again and looked down at Dolores's white face. She'd been a simple, young

Mexican girl who'd come to Texas to earn a fortune. In a few years, she would have gone home to find a husband and buy a ranch with the money she earned lying on her back. Pablo Contras found her down south somewhere and brought her to No Gap, as he had the other girls. He carried letters back to the families of those who could write.

Pablo was a strange man, Neemore thought. In Texas, he was a rancher, but in Mexico, his occupation was questionable. Who knew for sure what he stole or brought.

The light from the open door shone on the back path of the saloon. Neemore stepped sideways to enter the rear door.

"Oh, no." Rourke looked up from pouring the undertaker, Sloane, a drink. "Is it Dolores?"

Neemore nodded, unable to speak. The other girls came forward to view their dead sister by trade.

He stepped back and pulled out his watch. It was ten-thirty. Numbly, he went down the bar and picked up the drink that Sid poured for him.

The saloon owner had placed the Navy Colt beside Neemore's glass. The judge looked at the gun, his thoughts on the seven men in the jail. One of them might be Dolores's killer.

He turned to the women. His throat felt rusty as if he hadn't used it for a long time. "Who did this?"

The girls' blank eyes gave him no answer, and his impatience flared into a red-hot flame. "Who the hell did this to her? *Tell me!*"

"We — we think it was — ah — Curly," Roberta stammered.

The other girls nodded in agreement.

"Is he one of the boys in jail?"

The chorus of fearful nods from the girls gave Neemore his answer. The judge downed the whiskey and picked up the Colt.

Sloane and Rourke had been silent, but now the undertaker spoke quietly. "Your Honor, shall I bury the girl?"

"Yes. Get a priest and give her a decent burial."

"Oh, I will," Sloane assured him. His expression appeared strained as though he wanted to do more but did not know how or what.

"I'm sorry." Neemore apologized for his curt manner. He downed another drink then went outside.

After crossing the street and courtyard, he entered the courthouse. A light shone in the sheriff's office and cast a yellow glow in the hallway.

When Jesus saw the footsteps belonged to Neemore, he lowered the shotgun. A smile of apology crossed his face. "Sorry, *Señor.* I did not know it was you."

"That's all right." Neemore placed the heavy pistol on the desk, then looked at the prisoners. They slumped on the bunks and floor in alcoholic-induced sleep.

"They are no trouble."

"Which one is Curly?"

Jesus shrugged. "I do not know these *hombres.*"

"Go get me a couple buckets of water." Neemore refused to look at him.

"Oh. Are they thirsty?" Jesus asked, as if he had been neglecting his duties.

Neemore shook his head, his anger temporarily dulled. He removed two pairs of handcuffs from the drawer and gestured for Jesus to carry out his order. The Mexican shuffled away to get the water. As his footsteps died away, Neemore laid the handcuffs on the desk and turned toward the crowded jail cell.

"Which one of you is Curly?"

No one stirred for a moment. Then a muffled voice from beneath a *sombrero* spoke. "Who's asking?"

Neemore strode to the cell and eyed the occupants. "I'm the judge here, mister. Now, I aim to find out which one of you is Curly."

His voice held a razor's edge that sent the prisoners scrambling to bloody awareness.

A haggard youth looked up into Neemore's frigid eyes.

"I'm Curly."

"Get up here," Neemore ordered.

The cowboy shuffled leisurely to the cell door. A key clicked in the lock and Neemore gestured for Curly to come out. He relocked the cell door, then turned to view the weary man. Neemore's right fist lashed out and connected with Curly's jaw, taking the young man by surprise. The force sent him across the room and into the wall. He slid down with a stunned look covering his face.

"You son of a bitch!" Neemore's eyes cut to slits.

"What's wrong with you, Judge?" Curly cringed as the judge's boot connected with his leg. He held his hands up to protect himself.

"You know! You killed that girl!" The toe of his boot punctuated each word as he battered the cowboy.

189

"Tell me you killed her, you bastard. *Tell me!*"

Blinded by his anger, Neemore's foot continued stomping the man. He swung the heavy metal key ring repeatedly. His throat became scratchy from his loud curses. Finally, exhausted and out of breath, he leaned on the wall gasping for air.

Curly was a miserable whimpering huddle on the floor. His uncontrollable trembling made his body shake like a freezing dog. "She was just a gawdamn Mexican whore."

Neemore nodded in silent agreement and pushed himself off the wall. It was almost as if nothing had happened.

Curly raised to a sitting position and except for a cut lip and his ragged breathing, he appeared the same. Neemore picked up the long-barreled Colt. Curly's blue eyes flew wide and the color drained from his face.

The cell bars, which had been lined with on-looking ranch hands moments ago, were now empty. The occupants had retreated to the depths of their cell, their eyes downcast.

"Just a whore, huh?" Neemore drawled while cocking the Colt. His first shot was high to the right. Plaster splattered Curly, whose hands flew to his face protectively. A high-pitched scream left his throat. Gunsmoke fogged the room. Curly peeked through his fingers. Neemore's second shot dusted him down from just above his head.

"Just a Mexican whore, huh?" Neemore repeated as he fired the pistol at the wall near Curly's head. Each shot came closer and closer to the cringing man. The judge's eyes burned with hatred, but something kept him from lowering the barrel the scant inch and sending Dolores's killer straight to hell.

Finally, he laid down the smoking pistol. Wide-eyed, Jesus entered, sloshing water from two wooden buckets. "*Madre de Dios!* What is wrong, Judge?"

"Lock that killer up." Neemore pointed at the broken-down Curly. Then he turned and walked wearily toward the door.

Curly had not learned his lesson, apparently. "Charlie Brackeen will get you for this!"

Charlie Brackeen could roast in Hell.

Neemore didn't bother to utter his thoughts aloud. He was going home. When he moved outside, he briefly wondered what time it was. The moon was nearly in the west, and it would soon set. Josie would be sick with worry.

It was foolish of her to worry about an old drover-turned-judge. He could still handle the lot of them. Alex and his deputies were no help. Hell, if he had to be everything in this county, he might as well get paid all four salaries. He was going to speak to Brackeen when the rancher returned from San Antone. Some things needed to be settled.

At his home a few minutes later, Neemore climbed the front steps. When he turned the doorknob and stepped inside, he announced himself wearily.

Josie rushed out to greet him. "My dear, dear husband, are you all right?"

"Yes, Josie." He sat down to take off his boots, wondering if he looked any different. Did his loss show on his face? Jesus.

Yes, wife of mine, I'm all right. Why shouldn't I be? He carried on a mental conversation. *They murdered my Dolores and shot up Ben's place. I shot a drunken cowboy who went for his gun, and I came close to killing an unarmed man because he killed my lover. Yes, my dear innocent wife, I'm just fine.*

To hell with all of this.

Chapter No. 13

Lack of sleep numbed Jed's brain. Heat waves danced before his dust-burnt eyes. The bay horse snorted frequently, a sign that he, too, was spent. Both horse and rider were near the limits of their endurance.

He checked the sun and estimated it to be near ten o'clock. The distance remaining to Neal Smith's farm was only a few miles. Soon, he and the bay would be in the valley. Jed forced himself to stay awake and keep spurring the bay to continue.

Maybe he could sleep for just a few moments?

No! If he ever stopped, the horse would be too stiff to continue. The bay was a damned good horse, but he would probably be stiff-legged the rest of his life. He considered it shameful to have pushed his horse to that extent, but he felt it necessary in this instance.

Neal's dogs barked viciously, announcing

his arrival. Numb-headed, trying to rouse himself, he squinted his eyes against the sun. Was that Tell-her running towards him? The dancing heat waves blurred his vision and weighed down his heavy eyelids.

Sleep. Sleep. Sleep.

Jed gave way to the hypnotic sound and watched the world fade to black.

Later, when he awoke, everything was dark. A cool, wet towel lay across his burning forehead. With difficulty, he forced his eyes to focus. Neal Smith smiled down at him.

Jed licked his cracked lips. "Neal, I — I never killed Shoat."

"We already figured that out, friend. But, who did?" Neal seemed to be waiting for an answer that Jed couldn't supply.

He tried to sit up before he realized how weak he was.

"Just lie still. You've been through hell." Neal waited until he laid back against the covers. "Did you find out anything new?"

"A lot." Jed sighed. "Brackeen's gone to San Antone. Been there a while. Seems funny to me no one knew about that. His coming and going is usually public gossip."

Jed stopped to catch his breath and tried to summon some strength. The weariness consuming his body worried him. "Woodbridge and Buster are behind this crazy deal somehow. I eavesdropped on them last night and heard some things."

"You were *eavesdropping* on Brackeen's outfit? Did they catch you?"

"No. Otherwise, I guess I'd never have made it here. But I did have to tie up one of their guards, so more than likely they know I was there."

"What's all this mean, Pa?" Tell-her had moved behind his father to stare down at Jed.

"It means that more'n likely they'll never take Jed in alive — that's what it means! Shitfire, boy, you keep an eye out. We may all be in trouble."

Tell-her snorted. "They ain't sneaking past our gawd damned hounds."

Neal looked deep in thought. "What do you make of it, Jed? Charles Brackeen ain't never been away when there was trouble like this. That old bastard's been around, and he never trusted no one — not even Buster — to give more'n one day's orders at a time."

"Yeah." Jed nodded. "Buster and that old sheriff were cooking up something damned funny. I got an earful, and yet I didn't get enough information. Oh, yeah, I recall they said that the cattle are coming down here 'cause they're out of range grass."

He glanced beyond Neal to Mae, who was holding a steaming bowl of food, waiting patiently, her Cherokee eyes expressionless.

Neal turned as if he felt her presence, then scooted his chair over. "Eat something. I'll go get word to Sam and the others about the cattle coming. We sent word to Pablo to come, too. A Mexican boy rode out today for the border. The old devil's got a stake in this."

"It'll take Pablo a week to get up here." Jed sat up. He had mixed feelings about the bandit's return. One day he and that old crook would have bad words over Gabriella. Perhaps it would come down to using their guns, but Jed figured Pablo was at fault for leaving her alone so much. Besides, it was common knowledge that Pablo was living with some sweet thing across the Rio Grande whenever he was down there. Still, Contras did have a stake here. Some of the yearling steers Jed ran were in a partnership with him. Plus, Contras had his own stock at Gabriella's.

The soup Mae finally handed him was good, but he grew weary and full before he could finish it.

Neal rose. "Sleep awhile, Jed."

"I figure that Blythe and Wells are still

waiting outside Contras's place for me."

"They're probably still sleeping. Tell-her seen them this morning. One of them was on the south trail coming this way. He said the other one was snoring like an old hound. He left him sleeping and came on back here."

"Alex Woodbridge ain't sleeping." His head rested on the blanket, and his eyes grew heavier. Now that his stomach was full, and his mind was somewhat relieved, he drifted back to sleep.

When Jed opened his eyes again, it was still dark outside. A sense of urgency forced him up on his elbows. The dim light from the lantern on the table blinded his sore eyes.

A soft feminine voice spoke to him from the dark. "It's still Friday, Jed. Neal's gone to Sam's place."

Jed narrowed his eyes, then blinked in surprise when he recognized the owner of the unfamiliar voice, Mae. He couldn't ever remember hearing her speak before.

A small smile lifted her thin lips. "Tell-her is outside guarding the place."

"Mae, I'm sorry. It looks like I've brought you all into my mess. Course, you've crossed with Brackeen a time or two yourself."

Mae nodded and left the room. Jed drew

his legs over the edge of the bed and looked up to see that she'd returned with a cup of coffee. Wordlessly, she handed him the steaming cup.

He took a long drink. "I'll be leaving. Ain't no sense in you all being on guard for me."

"No." Mae shook her head. "If we back up now, Brackeen will run over everyone. He's tried that for years. It's about time we took a stand against him."

Jed studied the woman's strong face in the pale light. Her dark eyes were sharp and appeared to penetrate straight inside a person. Her coarse black hair was loose and flowed down her back. In the plain, brown dresses she wore, she looked thin, but her arms were nothing but hard muscle.

"You don't have much use for Charlie, do you?"

"Humph!" She snorted through her nose. "There's Charlie Brackeens everywhere you go. We had them at home. If people back up from them, they take more, so people back up some more. Soon the Brackeens of the world will own everything."

He couldn't argue with that. "All my life I figured he was the biggest, most powerful man in Texas. Nobody in Callie County but Charlie ever dressed as fancy as he does. He wore a white hat while the rest of the folks wore dirty ones. I went to San Antone when I was sixteen or so. Hell, everybody there had a white hat."

"I remember how he always looked down his nose at Neal in town."

"I've seen that look before." Jed found it hard to believe he was having this conversation with her. He knew the look she meant. The day Buster Deets roped him off his horse, Charlie had ridden over and glared down his thin nose at Jed's young face. The Texas sun blazed in his eyes, and the white Stetson created a halo around his head.

He sipped his coffee reflectively, trying to repress the old feelings of vengeance boiling in his gut.

"I've got some beans. Come to the table."

Jed rose and searched for his gun belt. His weapon was his first thought when he stood up. The Colt was his armor against the Alex Woodbridges, Buster Deetses, and Charlie Brackeens of the world. Since his late teens, Jed had always worn a sidearm. And now, he mused, it seemed the gun was his only security. He couldn't go home — he couldn't go to Gabriella's. It didn't matter about the dusty old house at his ranch, but Gabriella was a different matter.

He spotted the holstered gun on a kitchen chair and moved to pick it up. After unbuckling the belt, he strapped it on his waist. He shoved it down below his pants belt and hefted the Colt a few inches to test its position.

Mae stood watching him. "You know your beans are be getting cold."

He nodded and gave the gun handle a slap with his palm to secure it in the holster.

Mae smiled, her eyes crinkling. He knew staring at her must appear rude, but he couldn't seem to help it. She returned his look, then left the room. Jed sat at the table and studied the beans in the chipped bowl. He spooned his first mouthful, allowing his unconscious free reign.

First, she had carried on a normal conversation with him, then she had actually smiled. Strange, very different. The sound of boots broke through his thoughts. Jed looked up to see Tell-her coming in the front door.

"You get enough sleep, Jed?"

Before Jed could answer, Mae returned carrying another bowl of beans. She set it down across from Jed. Not meeting his eyes, she left the room.

He turned his attention back to Tell-her. "I got plenty, I guess. Anything going on outside?"

"No. Them hounds hear better'n I do at

night. If they catch a sniff of anything, we'll know it." Tell-her shrugged and gulped down some beans.

Jed ate his food slowly, allowing them to fill the void in his stomach.

Tell-her stopped eating long enough to speak again. "Shoat was no fool, Jed. Me and Pa figure a good hand with a gun got him. Gawdammit, he was a helluva brother." His voice trailed off, tears welling in his eyes. "The sumbitch who did it needs killing! I'm going to kill him myself."

"I understand, Tell-her." Jed could hardly speak over the lump in his throat. "Believe me, if I knew who was responsible, I'd do it myself."

"It's that damned Charlie Brackeen. That bastard's got to pay!" Tell-her scowled darkly. His head shook, and a muscle played in his jawbone. "I'll get him."

Jed nodded. There wasn't a lot he could say. Tell-her had a right to be angry, but Jed worried about what the boy might do in a moment of violent rage.

The dogs began barking, startling them.

"Who do you think that is?" Tell-her cocked his head and sat tense, his spoon paused in mid-air. He nodded, then swallowed the spoonful of beans. "It's Pa. I recognize Bugle's treeing bark."

"How in hell you can figure one dog's voice from the other is beyond me, but I'll wait and see."

"You won't need your gun," Tell-her rose. A moment later, he had the front door open.

"Relax, Jed. It's Pa and Sam and some others." Jed took his hand off the Colt's butt and joined the boy at the door.

"You guarding this place, boy?" Neal demanded.

"Hell, ain't nothing been here, and least I didn't shoot you, Pa."

"I said, by gawd, to guard this place," Neal grumbled as he strode past his son.

"Come on in, Sam. Tell-her, call your mom. Aw, here you are. Woman, fix these men some food." He turned to Jed. "Well, Jed, a bunch of Brackeen's crew was in No Gap shooting hell out of things."

"Yeah, with Alex up at the B-Bar-M and his deputies waiting for me, I guess all the law was gone, huh?"

Sam Allen took off his hat before he spoke. "Reckon so. I could tell when I left Swafford's store that it was pretty wild over at Ben's Saloon. And it wasn't even sundown yet."

Jed searched their faces for an answer. "What the hell were they doing in town in the middle of the week?"

"Good question." Sam smiled and shook his head.

"Swafford said he hadn't seen Blythe or Wells, so I guess they're still around Gabriella's place waiting on you, Jed."

Neal grinned. "They'll be grumpy when Woodbridge gets them to come back to town."

Mae set two plates of beans on the table and immediately left the room. From the corner of his eye, Jed watched her. He felt a small regret that she had returned to her silent manner.

"I figure it's a draw." Neal drummed his fingers on the table. "I'll bet they're moving cattle right now and want us to think every hand is in town. What do you think, Jed?"

He frowned, then nodded slowly. It was a real possibility. There had been cowboys sleeping in the bunkhouse the previous night. Brackeen was no fool, and it was like him to plan something like this. "You might be right, Neal."

Sam raised his brows and looked at both men in turn. "We heard that it got so bad Neemore had to shoot one of them hands in town."

Jed blinked in surprise and let out a low

whistle. "Judge Davis shot one? I never would have figured on that."

CHAPTER NO. 14

Neemore Davis had argued with his house-keeper and left the house in a black mood. He didn't usually go to the courthouse on Saturday, but he was anxious to see the absentee sheriff and get some answers. The soft light of dawn squeezed a yellow glow through the drab trees above. Birds gossiped on the branches, and a jackass brayed gruffly. But even the coolness of early dawn didn't soothe his anger.

He entered the rear door of the court-house, his heels pounding on the gritty wood floor. Even the sunlight that cut a yellow shaft down the hallway irritated him, coming as it did through the broken windows.

When he entered the sheriff's office and jail, he frowned. Some of the hungover cowboys were carrying a body out of the one of the cells. Neemore recognized the dead man's face — Dolores's killer, Curly.

The sheriff whirled at his footsteps. He scowled and looked accusingly at Neemore. "He hung himself. What in hell's name have you been doing, Davis?"

"I have a damned sight better question — where in *hell* have you been?" Neemore demanded. "These idiots shot up the whole damned town. That worthless bastard there strangled Dolores, and I had to play sheriff because your dumb deputies were out playing with themselves!"

Woodbridge let out a disgusted sigh. "Why didn't you just settle those men down?"

"I'll settle *you* down." He was so furious, he was having trouble breathing. "I want every one of those men in there fined for disturbing the peace, and I want them to pay Sid for the damage they did to his place."

"They were here to help me bring in Mahan."

Neemore shook his head, unmoved by the excuse. "Listen, for ten cents I'd have shot the whole lot of them and fed them to the buzzards."

"Well, you shot one, and that boy there was a good hand." Woodbridge pointed at Curly's body, now lying on the floor. "Besides, he was probably only funning with her, and she choked."

"Gawd damn you, Alex! You can do what you want, but if you *ever* leave No Gap without any kind of lawmen again —" Neemore had to stop himself because he was so close to doing Alex a physical violence. His fists ached from the tight grip he held.

"Neemore," Alex lowered his voice and spoke in a reasonable tone, "let's go in your office and discuss this."

The judge didn't trust himself to speak. He turned and stalked out the door. Loud spur rowels clanged behind him, so he knew Alex was following him.

After unlocking his office door, Neemore threw it back causing the frosted glass to rattle. Alex followed and stood glaring across the judge's desk. "Have you lost your mind?"

Swallowing back a sarcastic retort, he waited until the rage inside him lowered to a simmer. His eyes narrowed to slits, but he knew his anger was not overly upsetting to the hard-nosed sheriff. Finally, he drew a harsh breath and spoke slowly. "Alex, it don't make a damn whose idea this scheme was. It was a poor one. Those cowhands went wild! And that son of a bitch who hung himself was lucky he lived as long as he did."

"That Mexican you left to guard them

said you used Curly for target practice."
Woodbridge moved to the rear window.
"That's another thing, you shot hell out of
the west wall of my jail."

"So? Alex, tell me something — where's
your witness who says that Mahan shot the
Smith boy?" His anger had cooled enough
to allow him to think reasonably.

"He did it."

"No. that's not good enough." Neemore
shook his head gravely. "I want to know who
saw him do it."

"Couple of the cowboys, and they'll be at
the trial. Don't you worry. I'll have plenty
of proof. That sumbitch shot him, all right."

"Why?"

"Hell, probably over Pablo's wife. I think
Shoat was messing around over there, too."

"Then why in hell's name would Jed shoot
him fifteen miles away over at Dead Horse
Creek?"

"Listen, Neemore, I'm the gawdamned
law. You stick to being the judge. He'll get a
trial, and then we can hang him."

"Is Charlie back yet?"

Alex whirled on his heels. "What's he got
to do with this? I'm the law here. I don't
need you or Charlie Brackeen or anyone
else telling me how to handle my job."

Neemore watched him storm out of the

office. It was time to do something about this whole damned mess. Woodbridge had given his hand away by saying Jed would be hanged. He obviously had no intention of giving the boy a fair chance. Something was eating at the sheriff, but he wasn't taking Neemore into his confidences. The man was getting beyond anyone's control.

He checked his watch — seven forty-five. After snapping the lid shut, he dropped into his chair and studied the ledger-strewn desk.

A premonition flashed blurring before his eyes.

The vision caused him to make a firm decision.

He would have to keep a close eye on Alex. Jed Mahan had become a symbol of some kind to the sheriff, not unlike the pair of drifters he'd shot down over at Ben's Saloon. Mahan might not be a shining example of a gentleman, but he had friends. Woodbridge might be so blinded that he'd do something stupid.

Like gunning Jed down in cold blood.

Yes, he decided, as he polished his eye-glasses, he'd have to be on guard for any unpredictable happenings. With his ear cocked for activity across the hall in the jail, the judge turned to his open ledger. An hour passed, and he had done little more than glance at the entries, unable to clear his mind of the subject of Woodbridge and Mahan.

A loud clatter of horse hooves outside drew his attention. Someone was coming to the courthouse. When they drew nearer, he recognized the voices of Alex's two deputies, Wells and Blythe. Neemore rose and went to the doorway.

"That sumbitch ain't at the Contras place no more!" Blythe shouted as he entered the building. "And we got word that they sent for that goddamn old bandit Pablo."

"Who sent for him?"

"We spoke to some Mexican rancher on the road. He seemed damned tickled about it. I nearly slapped him."

Woodbridge punched the wall. "You stupid *ass!*"

Still unnoticed, Neemore moved in behind them.

Wells shook his head in disgust. "By gawd, Jed never came by either of us."

"Hell, no, he was tying up guards on the B-Bar-M while you two sat on your asses waiting for him to surrender."

Blythe blinked in amazement. "How in hell's name did he get up there?"

"On wings. Damnit, Blythe. I gave you

and Wells a simple job, and you came in empty-handed. This talk about them sending for Contras is just a bunch of shit."

Neemore knew if Pablo Contras did come, he could muster every tortilla twister in the county to help. Jed Mahan was in with the white ranchers, but Pablo could gather a Mexican army overnight. It was an inescapable fact, and it filled him with uneasiness.

"Well, we ain't waiting on that old devil." Woodbridge turned toward the last of the cowboys who had spent the night in the jail. "All you men go saddle yourself a horse. We're going out to get Mahan now."

Neemore cleared his throat. "Alex, leave one of those two deputies here. I'm going after my horse."

"What about that trial with that goat eater?"

"I ain't got time for that. Send someone down to tell Lupe that we'll settle it on Monday. This matter with Jed should be resolved by then."

Alex looked displeased, but agreed with a nod.

Neemore went back to his office and took the Navy Colt out of his drawer, along with some tarnished cartridges. The thought of riding a horse all day made his hip joints ache, but this was too important. He stacked his ledgers in a neat pile, then turned to check the green safe.

Preceded by the sound of his noisy spurs, Woodbridge came in. Neemore gave him a casual glance. "You ain't talking me out of going along with you, Alex. Someone with some sense needs to ride with you."

"Sense?" Alex's distaste for the word flashed over his face. He rubbed at his black eye patch and swore under his breath.

"You heard me. That bunch of wild men in there are drifters. I don't know where Charlie's old veterans are, but that bunch of kids are wild. I've seen them in action. And we ain't making no Sherman's March through south Callie County."

"What if — well, what if some state guy comes here?"

Neemore shook his head. "He can set on his rump and wait for me. I'll be ready in an hour."

"It's your sore ass." Alex held up his hands, surrendering to Neemore's determination to join the posse.

Neemore hurried home. He sent Rosalina's man to saddle up his bay horse, about the best one he owned. On his annual tax collection trips, Neemore rode him as often as he could.

Inside the house, he called to his wife.

Josie appeared at the top of the stairs, a flimsy duster wrapped around her. Obviously, she had just gotten out of bed. Neemore's eyes filled with admiration as he gazed upward at her. Whether that damned bedroom was hot or not, Neemore decided, when he returned, she would be sharing it with him.

"What's wrong, Neemore?"

"I'm going out with the posse to search for Jed Mahan."

Her eyes widened. "Oh my dear, dear man. Why must you go out? Don't you have deputies? What about Alex?"

"Josie, I have dummies and wild men under me. Someone had better use a little good sense or this county will be at war. The small ranchers have sent for Pablo Contras, and if he gets the Mexicans riled up and they join the ranchers, I don't know what will happen."

"I just hope the people of this county appreciate all you do for them. I'll get your raincoat." With that, Josie hurried off to the rear of the house.

Neemore smiled wryly. Only Josie would think of getting his raincoat when they were in the middle of a drought. He went to the closet and found a holster. After strapping it on, he changed into his boots. He gave Josie a smile when she returned triumphantly carrying his slicker.

"My, my, Neemore. You may just as well be sheriff, too, if you're going to do Alex's work."

"I'm just making sure Jed gets a fair shake." His mind raced ahead, trying to decide what he would need besides his bedroll. "Tell that housekeeper to wrap up some jerky for me."

"Goodness. Just how long do you suppose you'll be gone?"

He shrugged absently. A glance outside told him that Rosalina's man had brought the bay around front.

Rosalina shuffled out into the hallway ahead of Josie. *"Señor* Davis?"

Neemore closed his eyes, wondering what the quarrelsome woman wanted. "What is it?"

"What's this about Pablo Contras coming with an army?"

The judge studied her round face. Surprised at the genuine concern in her expression, he spoke casually to hide his own anxiety. "Why should that old bandit come back?"

She shrugged. "There is talk that he is coming."

"Well, let him come, then. We don't have

a problem with him, do we?"

"Maybe. Is this man Jed Mahan a big friend of his?"

"Oh, goodness!" Josie had hold of his sleeve. "Neemore, you will be careful, won't you?"

"Who told you Pablo was coming to rescue Mahan?"

"It's all over. Every Mexican in town knows about it."

"You tell them that Mahan will get a fair trial. You hear me? A fair trial. I will guarantee it."

After kissing Josie goodbye, he took the sack of provisions from his housekeeper and went outside.

Rosalina had been genuinely upset about Contras coming back at the head of an army. Maybe she was right. Perhaps the old goat *was* coming back this time. Pablo and Mahan *were* friends, after all. They shared lots of things . . . including the Mexican's wife, Gabriella.

Neemore tried to clear his brain. This business of arresting Mahan would have to be swift and clean.

By the time Neemore rode back to the courthouse, the B-Bar-M riders were saddled up and ready to go.

Alex swung up on a chunky bay and

215

waited for Neemore to join him. "I left Blythe and Wells here."

"Good. One can lose the other one," Neemore muttered under his breath. He glanced at the courthouse and wondered if it would still be standing when they returned. His last vision before they rode out was of the bowler-hat-wearing Blythe standing beside the bow-legged Wells on the front step.

Alex rolled a cigarette one-handed as he rode, then began identifying the members of the posse for Neemore. "The tall one is Francis. The little ones are Robert, Nelson, and Alf Dodd. William Stevens is riding the point, and Cliff Doone is the kid."

Neemore kept his voice low. "Where did Charlie get them?"

"Ft. Worth, I reckon. They're good hands."

"Sure." The judge wondered if Alex was trying to convince himself of the fact, too. Five hired cowhands as posse members, plus several men left back at the ranch, huh? As he rode along, Neemore estimated the cost to Charlie. Each man would cost twenty bucks a month, the price of a damned steer. Charlie's army was costing him plenty.

Neemore's bay trotted smoothly, but the dust the horses' hooves raised burned his nose. His hip was beginning to hurt already.

He checked his watch and found they'd been riding less than an hour. Sweat ran down his collar and from beneath his armpits. Being a member of the posse wasn't an easy job. He sure hoped that Jed Mahan appreciated him taking a part in the situation.

At least he would have tomorrow off. Alex wouldn't search for Jed on a Sunday.

Chapter No. 15

Early Saturday morning, Jed Mahan was still at Neal Smith's place.

"I'm going to check on Gabriella and make sure no one's bothered her," he told Neal and Sam Allen. "I'll keep a low profile. Maybe those deputies have given up by now."

Sam grimaced, his lips compressed tight.

Neal Smith spoke up. "We'll go up to Dead Horse Creek and make sure that Charlie ain't pushing his cattle south yet."

"And stay together." Deep concern furrowed Jed's brows. He knew Deets's plan was to pick the southern ranchers off one at a time as they had undoubtedly picked off Shoat. "I'll join you later on this afternoon up at Sheep Crossing."

Sam pursed his lips again and frowned. "They ain't liable to drive cattle down between Contras's place and No Gap, are they?"

Jed shook his head. "Country's too rough. It ain't nothing but a bunch of canyons and bluffs. No, the only way is by going through that west corridor."

"If it don't rain soon, there won't be grass down here for nobody's cattle." Neal shook his head warily. "Corn's going to burn up in our bottoms."

Jed nodded. Now that he had rested, he was anxious to be moving. He knew they should have a better plan formulated, but none came to mind.

Outside, Tell-her saw him and shifted the rifle cradled in his arms. "You leaving, Jed?"

"I'm going to meet you all later."

"You be careful. I wish we could get this all over with. It's plumb boring."

Jed looked at the youth and hid his smile. "I'll see you later, Tell-her." With a small salute, he went to catch his horse. There didn't seem to be a place where he could stay without jeopardizing someone.

Perhaps he ought to just ride on to Mexico — or hell, maybe somewhere even farther than that. The idea held little appeal, though. Besides, why should he run? He was innocent, and everyone knew it.

Everyone except a rigged Callie County jury might agree.

It was a possibility that sobered him. He

peeked at the sun from beneath the brim of his hat, judging the time to be somewhere around eleven o'clock. He stopped at the steep hill leading down to Gabriella's place. The dogs had already scented him and barked in excitement.

Gabriella was at the door, Winchester in her hands. He grinned and rode the bay down the steep incline.

"Jed!" Her bright red skirt swished around her shapely brown legs as she ran to meet him. Jed dismounted and swung her up in his arms.

Their hungry mouths met and savored one other. When he was out of breath, he slowly let her down. He searched her face, the glow in her eyes pleasing him. "Good. You're all right."

"Shh." She pulled him toward the house by the arm. Her warm brown eyes reflected in the sun as she looked into his face. "You were worried about me, yes?"

"Of course. Seems like everyone who helps me winds up in trouble." He stopped and pulled back from her efforts to usher him inside.

"Why do you not want me?"

Jed put his hand on her shoulders. "It's not that, Gabby. Woodbridge is up to more than just arresting me. If he had really wanted me the other day, he would've just waded in here. I think he wants a shootout, not an arrest. I suppose he figures I hold the ranchers together down here."

"Together? What do you mean?"

"Yeah. I guess Neal and Sam and the others have sort of picked me as the leader. So Alex wants me dead."

"No, no, no." She shook her head. "What can I do?"

"Stay safe. Pablo is coming home."

"Are you sure?"

"Yes." It hit him then that while he'd been talking to Gabriella, he'd let his guard down. His eyes darted around the canyon above them, aware that he could not afford to relax for a moment, not now. "Yes, the others sent for him."

"Jed, what will I do?"

"Well, I guess just be careful until Pablo gets here. This is his range, too. In fact, he has cattle that'll have to compete with Brackeen's for grass if they drive them down here. All the small Mexican outfits like Pablo and the others will join him if we have to fight."

She smiled. "I could get them to help you."

"Let Pablo lead them. I'm a danger to anyone."

"Come, let's go to my bed." She wrinkled her nose at him. Jed was tempted to do as she suggested. He slowly looked her over, and the memory of her naked body stirred him.

But he knew he didn't have time to indulge in his hunger.

"No, there will be time for that later. I have to get to the west and check on the others. I think the whole thing is a decoy to get everyone after me so Brackeen can drive cattle down here in our country."

"Bastardo." Gabriella spat out the ward. "I hope Pablo comes home and kills him."

"Well, you just keep that rifle close until that old bandit gets here." He lifted her chin with gentle fingers and pressed his lips against hers. For a moment, he reconsidered his options, but then dismissed the temptation to stay. "You be careful, Gabby."

She watched him mount, her eyes sparkling with tears. "Jed, please be careful. I will tell you something someday."

"What?"

She shook her head. "Nothing. Ride safely with the winds."

Jed raised his hand in farewell, then turned the bay around. He didn't trust himself to look back because he knew he might be tempted to go back and carry her to the high bed.

Why? Why was his life such a damn mess? On the run for a murder everyone knew he had not committed and in love with another man's wife. His life was hopelessly complicated, and he wondered if it would ever be simple again.

Neemore reined in beside Woodbridge when they reached Sam Allen's place. Et stood on the shaded porch. Neemore recalled that she could ride and rope like a man. She was definitely a rancher's wife.

"Mrs. Allen. We're going to have to ask you and Sam to help us." Alex cleared his throat. "Jed Mahan killed that Smith boy in cold blood."

Neemore watched the woman fling back her head in defiance, and her voice was scathing when she spoke. "Alex Woodbridge, I remember folks saying that you were a helluva Texas Ranger, once upon a time, but I figure you ain't nothing but a boot-licking cur now."

"You think what you like, Mrs. Allen. We're going to get that killer, Mahan." Woodbridge reined his horse around with a gesture to the other men to follow.

Et wasn't done, though. "There's folks around here who think you're through,

Woodbridge!"

Neemore smiled and touched his fingers to his hat. "Good day, Mrs. Allen."

The posse left at the same dust-rousing trot in which they had arrived. Neemore felt more and more like an outsider.

Alex's plan was for them to head west to Neal Smith's farm. Neemore was not going to pry into the sheriff's scheme. He was merely riding along to see justice was served. And that meant that he would not allow Woodbridge and his posse to kill Jed Mahan without the benefit of a trial.

A two-wheel cart loaded with firewood rumbled up the road. Alex raised his hand for the posse to halt as if he were some cavalry officer. The wagon was pulled by two skinny oxen, and walking beside the oxen was the goat-eater, Flores. Alex rode forward and spoke to him in Spanish.

Neemore understood enough of the language to know it was merely a greeting. Then Neemore detected Jed Mahan's name interspersed in the conversation several times. The judge clasped the saddlehorn and studied the woodcutter's dark face. When Alex mentioned the bandit Pablo Contras, a worried frown appeared on the old man's face.

Finally, Woodbridge turned away and

rejoined the posse. "Let's get on to Neal's place."

Neemore listened to the sparse words of the Brackeen cowboys. Perhaps, he decided, they were just wary of saying too much in his presence. They seemed very business-like on this errand of hunting Jed.

He shook his head. Eight against one were poor odds.

The Smith's son, Tell-her, had a rifle in his arms when the posse rode into the yard. A whole herd of hounds bawled at them in a throaty, threatening chorus. As the sheriff questioned the youth, Neemore studied the weathered house, ramshackle sheds, and barns.

"Tell Neal we aim to get Mahan and try him."

The boy's features gave nothing away. The judge noticed the small Smith woman appear at the door. A glint of metal reflected in the sun. The sight of the twelve gauge in the woman's arms filled Neemore with uneasiness. Her reputation with a sword was well known. No telling what she'd do with a gun. Should he ride up to warn Wood-bridge?

No need. Having noticed the scattergun, Alex nodded to the woman politely. "Mrs. Smith."

Mae stepped out on the porch, squinting her eyes at the posse. Neemore noted the hatred in her face and felt relieved that it was not directed at him. She turned towards him and spoke sharply, though. "Judge, you take this Brackeen scum out of here!"

She pointed the gun barrel towards the sheriff. "I kinda figured that he wants to hang Jed afore he's tried. He's in cahoots with Brackeen. But you, Judge Davis, are a good man who reads the law. You and I know that Jed Mahan never killed my eldest son."

Woodbridge snorted, hands resting on the saddlehorn. "That, Mrs. Smith, is something for the law to decide."

"No." Mae waved the gun barrel of the twelve gauge. "When I find out who killed Shoat, you won't need your old tin badge, Sheriff. And you won't need to read no law over him, Judge. 'Cause I'll kill him with my own two hands."

Neemore touched his hat politely, then turned his horse away, hoping Alex and the posse would follow suit.

Tell-her laughed after them. "Gawdamn it, Ma, go ahead and shoot 'em. You aim to, anyhow."

The youth's mocking laughter angered Neemore. The law of the county must have fallen hard to garner such disrespect. He spurred his horse and rode ahead of the others.

When this was over, things would be changing.

By the time the posse returned to No Gap, it was dark. Neemore was stiff and saddle-weary when they reined up in front of the courthouse. He was grateful to see that the county building was still intact.

The idiot — Blythe — looked out one of the broken windows. "That you, Sheriff?"

"Well, who else could it be out here?" When Woodbridge dismounted, his thin body seemed to sag.

"We going out again tomorrow?" Neemore's throat was dry and scratchy. He was afraid if he dismounted his legs would fold beneath him.

"Yes. Every day until we get him."

"Fine. Don't go without me." Ignoring the other men, he turned the horse for home.

In the darkness of his backyard, with only the crickets and cicadas to ridicule him, Neemore dismounted clumsily. After stripping off the saddle, he turned the horse loose in the lot. Neemore lowered himself down onto the edge of the horse tank and shook his head wearily. He wondered if saving Jed Mahan's hide was worth all the trouble he was going through.

By Monday, Neemore was growing accustomed to the stiffness of being in a saddle. He decided that Jed Mahan was probably squatted like a Comanche on some limestone bluff, probably peering from beneath the safety of some red cedars, laughing at the stupid posse.

Earlier in the morning, Alex had announced another plan. He called it, "The Sweep." Four of the posse members would be sent down the south slope, to the Contras's place, two others and Neemore would ride in the east way to her front door.

Why in hell that old outlaw Pablo stayed in Mexico was beyond Neemore. One look at Gabriella reminded him what a fine-looking woman she was — the type he could retire to Texas brush with and never come out. Her long hair was black as a crow's wing. Her big sleepy eyes lured a man, and her mouth begged to be kissed. Her supple body was as ripe as a melon and just as enticing. Neemore found her the highlight of his days in the saddle.

When Woodbridge asked Gabriella if Pablo was coming home, her answer was a flat, "If he does, I hope he kills you and those two deputies who come snooping around here."

Neemore grinned at her contempt. Other than one of the cowboys getting bitten by one of her dogs, it had been an uneventful stop. Neemore surmised that Jed either knew where the posse was, or else he was out of the county.

Alex sighed heavily when they rode back into No Gap. "I'm sending the cowboys home tonight."

He shrugged. "Sounds reasonable, since we've been everywhere with no trace of him. You going out tomorrow?"

"No, I'll send Blythe and Wells out. I don't believe that Mahan's left the country. He's got cattle and friends here — especially that Mexican bitch. He'll show up eventually."

Neemore was too tired to even speak. He was glad Rosalina's man, Diego, would be at home to put his horse up. As he jogged the bay homeward in the darkness, he weighed a plan of his own.

If he had the strength tomorrow, he decided, he would put it into action. Of course, he'd have to confide in Josie and Rosalina and Diego, but they were the only ones who would know what he was up to.

Diego stepped down from the back porch and came forward to take the horse's reins.

"Evening."

"*Señor,* did you hear about Pablo Contras?"

"No." Neemore sighed inwardly, wondering what new rumor had started.

"He is dead."

"What?" Neemore turned and stared at him in the dim light. "When did this happen?"

"Last week, I think. The *Federales,* they shoot him dead. A boy came back today with the news. They say Pablo Contras is a good *bandito.*" The rest of his statement was muttered in Spanish.

"Well, who will take his place?" Neemore asked absently, not greatly concerned about the bandit's demise. It was one thing less he had to worry about. Still, he could afford to be generous with his sympathy with this man. "Who will find the girls for Ben's Trace and new livestock for the ranchers? Old Pablo helped lots of people."

"*Sí,* he was a good *hombre* to the Mexican people around here." Diego lowered his head and slowly pulled the horse behind him.

Late Monday afternoon, Jed heard the news of Pablo's death from Gabriella. He held her in his arms, his eyes scanning the canyon above them. He had kept an eye on the posse's movements. The fact that Alex and Neemore were traipsing around together with six B-Bar-M hands was perplexing. He couldn't see the need for the judge to ride with them. Every day the posse had followed the same pattern, but Jed figured it was a ruse to get him to lower his guard, something he had no intentions of doing.

"Pablo is dead," Gabriella sobbed against his blue shirt. "A boy came today to tell me that the *Federales* shot him and all of his men."

A wave of remorse gripped him, quickly followed by relief. He comforted Gabriella as best he could, but the soft suppleness of her body created an ache inside him.

Pushing back her hair, he nibbled at her neck, but she did not respond. "Let's go to bed."

She looked up into his face, "I am just a widow."

Jed shrugged and spoke softly, "It's not as big a sin to love a widow as it is to love a wife."

"Yes, but — everything is different now."

Jed felt her resistance melt. He spoke against her temple. "How do you figure that?"

"Because." Her voice was a breathless

sigh. "Now, I can have your baby."

Stiffening in amazement, Jed blinked, then held her away from him. "*My* baby?"

"He would not come out. All that turpentine, and still he would not come out."

Jed shook his head in bemusement. He pointed at her stomach. "That's my baby in there?"

"Yes. But I could not have let Pablo know it was not his."

Stunned with a mixture of anger and delight, Jed sighed and looked around the dusky rangeland. Gabriella was a puzzling woman, but he suddenly realized she was also a very rich one if he could collect Pablo's debts for her.

And she was carrying *his* baby.

Later, they lay on the high featherbed, wrapped in each other's arms. Exhausted but relieved, Jed stared at the ceiling. His life had taken such a different turn in the past few weeks. Something definite needed to be resolved soon. He just hoped that, for now, the posse was in town sleeping. Things were beginning to look a little better for his future.

He lifted his hand and placed it on Gabriella's belly. A smile lifted the corners of his mouth, and a need grew inside him again. His final thought before he gathered her in his arms again was that, in the morning, he would ride out the back way and go check on his friends.

Chapter No. 16

At first light on Tuesday morning, Neemore Davis stood on the road heading eastward out of town. Diego sat on a sorrel behind him, holding the reins to Neemore's bay.

He stepped into the road and flagged down the mail wagon.

"Why, Judge Davis." The mail carrier, Pete Quinn, blinked in surprise. "What can I do you for?"

"I need a favor." Neemore stepped out of the path of a stream of tobacco juice the mailman spat out. "Take me to San Antonio, and don't tell a soul about it. It's worth twenty bucks to you."

"Hell's fire, for twenty bucks I'd take you to New Orleans and back. Get up here on the seat. Gawdamn, I can sure keep a secret." Pete laughed. He jerked his head in Diego's direction. "What about him?"

"Diego ain't talking." Neemore swung his carpetbag up into the back of the wagon and then levered himself up into the seat. He turned back towards the hired man. "Diego, I'll see you here in two or three days."

Diego nodded, turned, and lead the horse away.

Pete lifted the reins to the team. "Everything okay, Your Honor?"

"Fine. Will we get there late tonight?"

"Be closer to midnight or so."

"Whenever." Neemore nodded and shifted the heavy Colt at his waist.

Pete bounced on the spring seat as the horses picked up speed. "Where you going to stay in San Antone?"

Neemore gripped the iron rail to prevent himself from being thrown over the side. "At the El Rosa Hotel, I reckon."

"Road gets better," Pete promised as they both lurched about on the wagon seat.

Pete made three changes of teams at small ranches along the way. The families fed and cared for the horses cheaper than a livery would have. At each stop, Pete and Neemore feasted either on beans in *tortillas* or bread and cold fried bacon, followed by bitter coffee to wash down the heavy meal. The food didn't seem to bother Pete, and Neemore ate his without comment. There was no regular stage, so the only way to get to

San Antone was to ride or drive. Neemore wasn't complaining, because it could have been worse.

When Pete reined up on the busy brick street in front of the El Rosa, Neemore grunted in relief. His butt was sore, and his kidneys felt shaken loose.

"I'll want to go back probably Friday," Neemore told the mail carrier.

"I'll be here, Judge." Pete handed down the carpetbag, spit over the side of the wagon, then drove his horses off.

Neemore climbed the low steps of the hotel and went into the lobby. He checked in, and a few minutes later followed the boy who carried his bags up to a room on the second floor.

Tomorrow he would find Charlie Brackeen and discuss the Callie County problems with him. It just wasn't like Charlie to den up somewhere this long.

It was past midnight when Neemore checked his watch, then blew out the lamp. All he wanted now was some rest. He settled on the hard bed to pull off his boots, expecting the bed to buck him off or rock sideways. When it did neither, he sighed in relief and proceeded to undress. His head pounded, and he wished for a good swig of whiskey — something he had omitted when he packed for the trip.

At sunup, he opened his sleep-matted eyes and glanced around. After dressing hurriedly in a fresh shirt and yesterday's britches, he went down to the hotel restaurant. A quick cup of coffee rejuvenated his spirits.

Charlie's townhouse was only a few blocks from the hotel. Along the way, Neemore passed vendors hawking tortilla-rolled meals. He dodged freight wagons, burro trains, and livery wagons in the street.

At Brackeen's iron-grilled gate, Neemore wrung the bell. It would be yet another hot day. The night air had barely cooled the temperature from yesterday.

A round-faced man appeared at the gate. He looked at the judge suspiciously, "Yes, *Señor?*"

"Judge Neemore Davis here to see Mr. Brackeen."

"I don't know, *Señor* —" the man began.

"Who is it, Juan?" a cultured voice in the courtyard called.

"A Judge Davis, *Señor* Thornton," the man shouted over his shoulder.

"Well, show him in."

"Come in, *Señor,*" Juan offered, his face still troubled.

A small Anglo man in a fancy-dancy suit

offered his hand. "Good day, Judge Davis. It's a pleasure to meet you. I'm Parker Thornton, Mr. Brackeen's attorney."

Neemore frowned at the stranger. He had never heard of the young attorney. For that matter, he wasn't aware that old Charlie even *had* an attorney.

Deciding to keep a sharp eye on the man, Neemore stretched his hand out. "Mr. Thornton, I really came to see old Charlie."

"Judge Davis, I'll have to be honest with you." He paused seeming to try to read Neemore's expressionless face. "Charlie is not well. He really shouldn't be receiving any visitors. The doctors are doing all they can, but it doesn't look good."

"I see."

Thornton smiled with his mouth, but not with his eyes. The young man seemed determined to block Neemore's efforts to see Charlie. "However, I assure you, I've been given full authority to handle his business and legal matters."

Charlie Brackeen sick? Bullshit. Why, that old devil hadn't seen a sick day in his life. No, he wasn't swallowing that tale — not without the evidence of his own eyes.

The attorney guided him to a shady spot in the courtyard and gestured him toward a wicker chair. The high-plastered wall shut out the city. Walnut and pecan trees formed a canopy over a manicured lawn and garden.

Parker seated himself across from Neemore and asked politely, "Have you had breakfast?"

"Yes, thank you."

"Fine. I'll order some coffee, or would you prefer whiskey? You look like a whiskey man to me."

Neemore shook his head. "Coffee will be fine." He watched the young man as he called the round-faced Mexican over and ordered the coffee. The attorney was no fool, Neemore surmised. But his smooth manner and polite facade didn't faze him. It was just going to be a matter of time before Neemore found out what the man's game was.

"What's going on back in Callie County?"

"It's hot and dry."

"Yes. Mr. Deets reports that it is particularly difficult on the range grasses."

"Mr. Thornton, there has always been a south line for the B-Bar-M range. Dead Horse Creek was the dead line. Lately, it seems there have been incidents between Charlie's people and the ranchers south of the line." Neemore spoke slowly, laying his cards on the table. He had played enough poker to note any change of expression.

239

There was no change in the lawyer's face.

"Is there a legal precedent for this line, Judge Davis?"

"Can't really say, Thornton, but there are some established ideas in people's minds."

The lawyer shrugged. "So, we have a conflict. No doubt it can be settled in your court."

Neemore was having a difficult time restraining his temper. The glib-tongued lawyer was now making the "dead line" issue a legal one, dropping the matter in the county judge's lap. "It may be settled out there in the brush."

The coffee arrived, and Thornton poured the steaming liquid into bone china cups, then handed one to Neemore.

After a moment, Thornton placed his cup on the table, then steepled his fingers together. "Well, I can hardly see how this would affect the Brackeen ranch. Your Sheriff Woodbridge will just have to protect our interests."

Neemore did not miss the proprietorial "our" in the man's smug announcement. He looked innocently into the lawyer's eyes, "And, who, may I ask, will inherit the B-Bar-M if old Charlie dies?"

Thornton cocked a silky brow, but otherwise, did not seem perturbed by the question. He shrugged and waved a negligent hand. "Oh, various relatives who are provided for in his will."

Neemore peered at the man from beneath his shaggy brows. And he said to himself, *you, Parker Thornton, will receive a fat fee for administering the estate. And you'll live in this fancy townhouse, just in case any relatives come calling.* Well, ain't that some irony for old Charlie Brackeen who fought Comanches, border trash, rustlers, and thieves, and had done it all so that a pipsqueak of a lawyer could reap the benefits.

"What's really troubling you, Judge Davis?"

"I would like to see old Charlie before I go back home," Neemore said with an edge of determination that the lawyer couldn't miss. "We've been pretty close all these years."

"Very well," Thornton agreed. "But we mustn't disturb him about the small incidents in Callie County. You do understand, I'm sure?"

Neemore nodded. "I won't worry him."

"Finish your coffee, then we'll go to his room."

Neemore sipped the coffee slowly, his thoughts wandering. This townhouse and courtyard were a good place for an old

241

warhorse like Charlie to spend his last few days. Josie would have loved it.

"Ready?" Thornton asked a few minutes later. The house was cool and quiet. Neemore caught a glimpse of fine furniture before they ventured up the carpeted stairs.

Thornton rapped lightly on a heavy oak door. A nun answered his knock. Beyond her in a high bed, Neemore could see a pale, thin figure among the snowy, white sheets.

A hoarse voice welcomed Neemore. Charlie's slow smile seemed pained. "Hello, Neemore. W-what brings Callie County's judge here to my place?"

"I came to tell you to hurry up and get well, Charlie." Neemore swept off his hat and moved to the bedside.

"It's good to see you, Neemore."

The cold hand beneath his own shocked the judge. Charlie's sharp, blue eyes were milky and sunken, the skin across his protruding jaw bones almost transparent.

"I reckon if you'd get some rain, things would be all right up home, huh? How's your Josie?"

"Oh, fine. You know Josie."

Charlie nodded weakly. "A real lady. Yes, she's a real lady. Tell her I sent my best, will ya, Neemore?"

"I will. She'll be wishing you were up and

around."

"Fourth of July's coming up, ain't it? We need to have a popping good time this year."

"We will." Neemore lied uncomfortably. He could see the life draining out of Charlie's body a drip at a time.

"Yeah, you and Alex handling things fine, ain't you?"

Neemore nodded reassuringly. He wanted to get out of the room. Seeing Charlie in such a state was pathetic. His condition reminded Neemore of an old horse he had ridden as a boy. The horse had been turned out on the range. Later, Neemore ran across the horse again. His muzzle was gray with age, and he was so stiff he could barely shuffle from the grass to the water. The hide hung from his exposed ribs. Neemore had finally shot the old boy and put him out of his misery. Luckily, Charlie didn't expect the same treatment.

"Alex came by a month or so ago." Charlie wheezed. "He's a tough old bastard for his age. He's nearly as old as I am, but he's still going strong."

"Yes, sir." Neemore gave him a small smile. "Thornton said I could only stay a little while."

"I understand."

Neemore reflected sadly on their conversa-

243

tion. They both knew it had all been pretense. Charlie would never see another Fourth of July celebration. He rose and looked numbly at the old ranching king. "You take care, Charlie. I'll tell Josie you still love her."

"Yeah, you do that, Neemore," Charlie agreed, as if he suddenly realized it was true.

Neemore waved goodbye, then went out into the hall. He rested against the cool wall and looked out the window down at the courtyard. Thornton was handing an envelope to a boy. A letter? It would go on the mail run tomorrow. Maybe young Parker had written to Alex or Buster.

Well, he would just have to investigate the matter.

Wearily, Neemore went downstairs and then out into the courtyard. He replaced his Stetson and crossed to where Thornton sat.

"Well, Judge Davis? He's getting the best medical care available, as you can plainly see."

Neemore acknowledged the defensive comment with a nod. "Thanks, Thornton, I'll be going now."

"No need to rush off, Your Honor. We'll have lunch. Rest here."

Neemore had no intention of remaining in the smooth character's company. He cast a look upstairs. Now he knew why Alex had never mentioned being here. The man upstairs, like Woodbridge, had always been strong and healthy. Besides, Buster Deets and Alex might well be in cahoots with this milky-mouthed lawyer.

There was a helluva lot to sort out. Neemore knew he would be able to think clearer away from this place. "No. Thanks, anyway."

"Is something troubling you, Judge?"

"No. Just Charlie."

"I see. Well, if you really can't stay, then I'll see you out."

On the street again, Neemore breathed in a deep gasp of air, feeling as if he had been released from prison. He accepted the fact that he could do nothing for Charlie Brackeen. Thornton would have his way.

The same was not true for Jed Mahan.

Neemore looked up and down the brick street. There were two things that would help him right now — women and whiskey. The idea of getting drunk in a hotel room was not particularly inviting. On the other hand, a sporting house might not be such a bad way to spend the day. His decision made, Neemore breathed the clean air again and set off down the street.

The next morning in the pre-dawn light, the judge flagged down the mail wagon. He loaded his bag, then climbed in beside a surprised Pete.

"Thought you were going back tomorrow?"

"Changed my mind."

"Have a good visit, Judge?" Pete asked as he sped the team on their way.

"Yes." Neemore smiled in reminiscence. He recalled the pleasurable way he had spent part of the night. The girl's name had been Rebecca. She drawled like a Georgia Belle, and Neemore hadn't minded the fact that she was taller than him. Her pale skin glowed like polished ivory, and she had an elegant manner that surpassed any other woman he had known. And she had moaned the whole time, he recalled with a grin. Oh, could she moan.

Pete pushed the team around a wagon, then cleared his throat for Neemore's attention. "You was here on business, you said?" The man was obviously set on making conversation to help cover the long miles.

"Right. By the way, did you see a letter for Sheriff Woodbridge in the mail for No Gap?

"I think so. Why?"

"It may be a legal matter." He turned his

head sideways and spoke seriously. "You do know that a judge has the right to confiscate evidence, even if it's in a mailbag?"

"Evidence?" Pete repeated in bewilderment.

"Never mind. I'll pay you two bucks to give me the letter and shut up about it."

"Right. Evidence."

Neemore wondered about the letter. It certainly was a coincidence. Imagine, Neemore chuckled silently, that young snot Thornton thinking he was such a high and mighty smart thing. Hell, he wasn't half as cunning as he thought he was, tangling with an old fox like Neemore Davis.

It was almost dark when Neemore and Pete arrived at the small spread where Pete always spent the night. It was five miles short of No Gap. A small rancher by the name of Bob Rogers, along with his wife and a passel of children, lived in the adobe house. In the morning before daylight, Pete would deliver the mail to Swafford's Mercantile, then he'd head back to San Antone.

Neemore noted with surprise that Diego was waiting at the Rogers's ranch for him. Perhaps Rosalina's man would not be such a bad employee, after all. He obviously knew Pete's route and had taken it upon himself to come and meet the judge a day early, since Neemore hadn't been sure just how long he would be gone.

"Howdy, Judge Davis." Bob Rogers waved.

Pete spit out a stream of tobacco. "You ain't seen, His Honor. It's a court matter — kinda secret-like. You savvy, Bob?"

Rogers blinked his eyes, then beamed broadly. "Never seen you, sir."

"Thanks." Neemore handed his carpetbag to Diego, then mounted the bay.

The pair rode off in the darkness. They did not speak until they had traveled almost a mile.

"What's the news?" Neemore asked wearily.

"Old Pablo's widow is getting the Mexican ranchers to ride with her."

"She is?"

"Many Mexicans are ready to ride when she sends word."

"What the hell for?"

Diego lifted his head to study the shadowy night. "They say *Señor* Brackeen is pushing lots of cattle down here."

"Good grief. What's Woodbridge doing about it?"

"Nothing. He is looking for *Señor* Mahan still."

"Hell, let's get home. I need to recover from my illness."

In the quiet night, he reflected on the letter to Alex that Pete had fished out of the mailbag for him. As Neemore suspected, it was from Thornton. He had read it each time Pete stopped to rest the horses. The curt words were planted in his memory.

Alex,
I have no idea what Judge Davis is doing here. He came to San Antonio on a mission of some nature. He will bear close watching.
I fear our good judge may well be asking the wrong kind of questions.

CHAPTER No. 17

While riding with Tell-her to the Smith ranch, Jed had nearly run straight into Blythe and Wells. He and Tell-her sat in the seclusion of a cedar thicket, waiting for the deputies to ride on past. Earlier, Jed had seen a large dust cloud. He had a suspicion that Brackeen's men were going to scatter as many as a thousand head of cattle across the head of Horse Creek.

Closer inspection verified that suspicion.

"Whew! That was one damn close call." Jed held his hand over his horse's nose so it could not snort or whinny at the deputies' mounts.

"Yah." Tell-her cocked his head and squinted his eyes, listening for their fading horse hooves.

Through the branches of the trees, Jed spied the moving dust cloud. Wiping his sweating face on his sleeve, he mumbled, "I sure hope Gabriella's all right. If she has the small Mexican outfits ready to ride, we can get Sam and the others and turn those damned cattle back."

Tell-her rose and peered down the trail. "I think we can go on now. Those two deputies never saw or heard us."

"Good. Let's go."

They crossed the dried grassland bisected by the road, then urged the horses into the cover of more brush.

It was near dusk when the pair reached the Smith place. The dogs began barking loudly, bringing Neal Smith out on the porch with his shotgun.

"It's us, Pa!" Tell-her shouted. "We got lots of B-Bar-M cattle coming this way. Ain't we, Jed?"

"Yeah. I'll ride on over and tell Sam and the others."

"No, I'll do that, Jed." Neal waited until they had joined him on the porch before he spoke again. "Did you see them two deputies? They've been snooping around again."

"See 'em? We nearly run over 'em." Tell-her guffawed and shook his head.

Neal led the way inside the house. "Jed, there's no need of you taking any more chances. Let's eat, then I'll go get Sam and the others."

Jed agreed. He was worried about Ga-

251

briella, anyway. "I'll go see about Gabby. We may need all the help we can get. I figure Buster Deets is coming with his guns loaded."

Frowning, Neal nodded. "Yeah, them Mexicans will fight. They got a stake in this same as us."

They sat down at the table and began on the heaping plates of food Mae had provided.

"You think Gabriella can get them to ride with us, Jed?"

"Yeah, they all owe her late husband."

Tell-her clicked his teeth. "Poor Old Pablo. All them years down there, but the *Federales* finally got him."

Jed continued to fill his mouth with food. He had no comment to make about Gabriella's dead husband. His primary concern right now was her safety. She had become as important to him as the fight to uphold the "dead line."

Neal swallowed a bite. "After we settle this thing with Brackeen, what're you going to do, Jed? You can't keep dodging Woodbridge. Sooner or later he'll catch you, and we both know he don't aim to take you in to stand trial."

"I know, but I'm not ready to tuck tail and run. If there really was a law here, I'd turn myself in. I ain't decided yet just what Neemore's game is. Seems funny, him riding with that posse." He'd concluded long ago that to turn himself in to Alex would be suicidal.

Neal looked up from his food and squinted as if reading his thoughts. "Don't even think about turning yourself in. We'll figure something out after we've cleared up this range war."

"I hope so. I swear, Neal." Jed looked the rancher directly in the eye, "I never seen Shoat that night he was killed."

"Hell, Jed, we know that," Tell-her put in. "But somebody sure as hell saw him and shot him in the back."

Silence fell upon the room. Jed finished his food then stood up. He glanced at the rancher's silent wife. "Food's good, Mae. Thanks." Turning back to Neal, he said, "I'll go get Pablo's army ready to meet us at Dead Horse Creek at sunup. You get Sam and the others."

Neal jabbed the air with his fork. "You be careful. It could be a trap."

"I know." He hitched his holster and hurried out to his horse, anxious to be on his way to Gabriella's.

A few hours later, when he arrived there, the dogs were barking. Jed listened as the horse picked his way over the familiar trail in the dark. There were lights on in the windows. The lamp in the back bedroom was his signal that it was clear to ride in. Sagging with relief, he removed his hand that rested instinctively on the Colt's grip. When he reached the clearing at the bottom of the hill, he saw some silhouettes.

He stopped the horse and dismounted. Colt drawn, he advanced slowly down the last yards to the floor of the canyon. When the figures came into view again, they were all wearing *sombreros*. A wave of relief washed over him.

"*Señor* Mahan?"

Jed tensed, then realized that the dogs would have given him away. At least the voice was Spanish.

"Yes?"

"It is all clear. I am Raul Ramirez. Pancho is with me."

"Good." Jed holstered his pistol and stepped into the pale light from the windows.

"Where have you been?" Gabriella demanded as she ran out to meet him.

"Watching Brackeen's men gathering a lot of cattle. Let's all go inside." He followed Gabriella and the two Mexicans inside the house to the kitchen.

"So, when do they come?" Raul asked.

Jed took the cup of coffee she handed him before answering. "Midday tomorrow. They'll come across the creek."

"Ah. We will go get the rest of our people. How many men do they have?"

"At least fifteen, maybe more."

The rancher smiled confidently. "We have that many rifles, maybe more."

Jed frowned and looked into the handsome Mexican's face. "I'd rather no one got shot, but it'll be push or get shoved, I guess. They're coming for business this time."

"We thank you, *Señor* Mahan. We are very sorry about your trouble with the law, but it will be straight some time, we hope."

"Thanks. We'll all meet at Sheep's Crossing at sunup. Sam Allen, the Petersons, and Neal Smith and his son will be there," Jed assured the men.

"Be careful, *Señor* Jed." Raul nodded to the silent Pancho, and after a grin at Gabriella, the two men left.

Jed put down his coffee cup and, turning to her, he held out his arms. She melted against him, burying her face in his shirt.

"Oh, Jed. I am so worried."

He sighed heavily and ran a gentle hand down her hip.

"We'll be all right, Gabby. Tomorrow, all

this will be done with, and we can get on with our life."

Neemore rode the bay to the courthouse on Saturday morning. Diego had told him Woodbridge had been unsuccessful in arresting Jed Mahan during his absence. Three horses were hitched to the rail out back. He knew the dun belonged to Alex. The judge tied his horse beside the dun, then climbed the steps to the courthouse. Voices came from the sheriff's office, but when Neemore appeared in the doorway, silence fell.

Blythe looked up with a start. "Well, you feeling better, Judge? We got word that you were at home laid up sick." Neemore didn't bother to answer the question. With eyes hard as steel, he spoke with grim authority. "You and Wells get outside, Blythe. Me and the sheriff have some things to discuss."

The deputies looked at each other, then rose quickly and left the room.

"Well." Woodbridge leaned back and put his boots up on the desktop. "What is it this time, Neemore?"

"You went to see Charlie Brackeen a month ago?"

Alex shrugged carelessly. "So?"

"You've never said he was in San Antone,

or that old Charlie is ready to kick out of this world."

Alex fingered his black eye patch but turned away under his sharp gaze. "You must figure you have something that's important."

He stepped inside the office. "Well, I've been to see him and that shifty lawyer, Thornton."

Alex turned and looked up in surprise, then shrugged.

Neemore continued, his voice laced with sarcasm. "Kind of ironic that old Charlie worked all his life, so some city-slicker lawyer can get it all."

"Hell, Neemore, we all got to die sometime, and we can't take it with us. You know that."

"Yeah, we gotta die." He was sickened by the man's indifference. Alex had claimed to be Charlie's friend for years, and now he was probably the one behind Thornton's game to gain control of Charlie's estate. Neemore choked back an accusation and changed the subject. "You riding after Mahan again today?"

Alex nodded and rose. He went to the gun cabinet and gazed at the weapons on the rack. "Yeah, we've got word he's going to be above Sheep's Crossing on Dead Horse

Creek. I'll get him today. One way or the other, I'll get that young bastard."

Neemore heard the threat in Alex's muttered words, and his blood chilled. "I'm going with you."

"Ain't no need."

"Alex, don't you leave without me. I mean it. I'll be there when you catch up with Mahan."

Alex reached inside the gun cabinet and lightly stroked a Winchester stock. "Have it your way, Judge Davis."

"I intend to." Neemore turned and went to his office.

It wasn't long before Blythe stuck his head inside the door. "We're ready to ride, sir."

Neemore checked his watch. It was nine twenty-five. In a couple of hours, perhaps all this Mahan mess would be over.

The posse, headed today by Woodbridge and both his deputies, were mounted and waiting when Neemore brought his horse around front.

He nodded at Alex, then fell in with the line of men. Alex rode ahead of the group. Riding between Blythe and Wells, Neemore kept his eyes open, anticipating trouble at any moment. He'd heard enough, "By, Gawd, we'll get him today!" to last him a lifetime. If it hadn't been so much trouble, he would have stuffed a kerchief in both of their mouths.

Squinting under his Stetson, Neemore made out rising dust ahead.

The cloud grew as he watched. Someone was driving a large herd of cattle. Neemore twisted in the saddle and looked at their backtrail. His eyes widened in surprise at the storm clouds building up in the sky. They were coming from the distant gulf, a good sign. It was the first time in months that tall gray clouds had gathered in the sky, and they didn't appear to be passing, either. Neemore smiled as he realized he had ridden off without his slicker. Hell, maybe it really would rain.

Turning back, Neemore shouted to Woodbridge, "Who's moving all those cattle, Alex?"

"B-Bar-M."

"They're really going across the creek, huh?"

Alex didn't bother to turn as he answered, "It's a free country, Judge. They ain't breaking no law."

Blythe suddenly swore "Holy shit!"

He pointed south to a high ridge.

On a distant rise sat over two dozen riders. Armed riders, to boot. And the cattle were getting close. Neemore could hear the distant bawling north of the creek.

Woodbridge reined up, bringing the posse to a halt. Loud voices could be heard in the valley.

Buster Deets's gravelly voice echoed down to them. "Clear them bastards out, Mahan! My cattle are coming through!"

"Alex," Neemore said sharply, "you'd better get your ass down there. We're fixing to have a bloody war here."

"I told you there ain't no law —"

Neemore had had enough. "Gowd damn it, sheriff! Get down there and do your job. We ain't having no damned war."

Alex spurred his horse down the slope in the direction of the shouting. Neemore was close behind him.

A woman suddenly screamed a warning. "Jed! Watch out. It's the sheriff!"

Neemore looked around wildly. He spotted Gabriella riding hard from the south ridge. He jerked around to check Alex, but he was too late.

Alex's gun blasted at the man facing Buster Deets. It was Jed Mahan. Jed was hit and went over the side of his horse. Woodbridge re-cocked his pistol, but Jed's horse was in the way, preventing the sheriff from taking another shot. Neemore sent up a quick thanks that Jed's army was too far away to begin shooting.

He spurred his bay to catch Alex.

Jed's argument with Buster Deets had been a futile one that could end only one way, and that was in bloodshed. He suddenly heard Gabriella's warning cry when the hot lead cut across his shoulder. Then he'd dived for the ground.

The frightened horse seemed unsure whether to break the ground tie or not. Jed felt for his Colt, but found his holster empty. There was nothing he could do now but surrender.

On his lathered horse, the sheriff came riding hard, intent on nothing else but shooting him.

The irony of the situation was laughable. It looked like he was going to die not more than a hundred yards from the site where Brackeen's men had roped him off a horse twenty years ago.

Seemed like Charlie Brackeen's final lesson would come any moment now.

A shot rang out. The sheriff's gun went off in the air as he sprawled out over his galloping horse's head. Alex Woodbridge fell facedown to the ground, while his panicked horse bolted away.

Jed looked up to see Judge Davis's smoking, long-barreled pistol. He shook his head in bewilderment as Davis rode past the prone sheriff to the wide-eyed Buster.

"Get those damn cattle back north, Deets. You know where the line is. And another thing, you either control them cowboys in my county, or I'll control them for you."

Buster Deets scowled at Neemore. "I don't know what Mr. Brackeen's going to say about this."

"Don't you mean Thornton, Parker Thornton?" Neemore asked with contempt. "Hell, he ain't big enough to wear Charlie Brackeen's boots. Get them cattle turned — *now!*"

Jed half sat up as Gabriella dabbed at the bleeding streak the bullet had cut in his left shoulder. He glanced over her head at Blythe and Wells. They were carrying the sheriff's body between them. The look on their faces was one of sadness and shock.

Alex Woodbridge was dead.

Judge Davis returned from across the creek. Jed's army had gathered around him and Gabriella. Neemore looked warily at the grim-faced ranchers. They looked as they had back at the courthouse that day the windows had been shot out.

Neemore dismounted and walked over to him. "You all right, Jed?"

Jed nodded, satisfied he wasn't bleeding badly.

Neemore turned to the ranchers. "Well, those cattle ain't coming. I told Deets that this was the line. As for the charges against Jed here, I'm dropping them right here and now."

A cheer went up from the collected ranchers.

Neemore continued, a smile playing at the edges of his mouth. He checked his watch — eleven-thirty exactly. "Callie County needs a new sheriff. Jed, you think on that. I think you'd make an excellent candidate. And I'll be running for county commissioner and judge again this fall. I sure would appreciate your vote."

Neemore noted the nods of approval. He glanced at Jed, envying the attention Gabriella was heaping upon him. A drop of rain splashed on his face. He heaved a sigh of relief and moved off toward his horse.

It was time to go home to Josie.

Two days later, Neemore received a letter. Charlie Brackeen had died of a stroke at eleven-thirty, two days previously.

The day that it rained in Callie County.

Epilogue

Neemore Davis came down the hall wiping the sweat from his forehead with a handkerchief. He entered the sheriff's office without knocking. "Jed, you going out to the B-Bar-M for the Fourth?"

"It's not the B-Bar-M anymore."

"Oh, of course not. I just haven't got used to the new brand yet, is all. So, are you going?"

"I reckon so, if Gabby's feeling up to it. Why?"

"Well, I ordered that carryall for Josie's birthday and she's just itching to take someone for a ride in it. I was wondering if you and Gabriella might want to go with us."

"We'd be honored, Judge. I'll have to tie my horse to the back in case there's any trouble I need to handle, but the ride would sure be easier on Gabby. I appreciate it."

"Fine. That's just fine. I'll let Josie know."

Neemore turned with a big smile and headed back to his own office, wiping his brow again.

"Uh, Judge?"

"Yes, was there something else, Jed?"

"I'm thinking, hot as it is, I may stop by Ben's for a beer on the way home."

"A fine idea, Jed. I believe I'll join you. Just let me lock up and get my hat."

Jed shoved the sheaf of papers he'd been working on in a drawer, pushed back his chair, and stood. Out of habit, he checked the loads in his Colt and tucked the hammer loop safely behind the holster before turning to his deputy.

"Tell-her, I'm going to have a beer and take a turn around town before I go home. If you need me, you know where to find me."

"Yes, sir, Sheriff. I'll be right here or taking my own turn about until things settle down tonight. I'll be fine."

"I know you will, Tell." Jed plucked his hat off the peg by the door and headed for the judge's office.

Jed and Neemore got their beers from Sid and settled into a table in the front corner of the saloon. They talked quietly about county business and range conditions while sipping their suds. The batwings pushed open and two cowboys came in. Their hats and chaps immediately identified them as Texas riders.

Jed watched as they approached the bar.

"Two shots of rye and a couple of beers, barkeep," said the older of the two, laying a coin on the bar.

"Them boys look pretty rough," said Neemore. "The older one 'specially looks like he's got the bark on."

"I'll speak to 'em." Jed pushed his chair back. He walked over to the bar and leaned his left elbow against it, facing the two men. "You boys just passing through?"

"Who wants to know?" replied the youngster.

"My name's Mahan. I'm the sheriff here."

"I'm August Tarrant, Sheriff." The older one stepped up. "This here's my brother, James. He didn't mean no disrespect. Just gets a little proddy when he's hot and dry."

"No offense taken, Mr. Tarrant, but my question remains."

"You know how it is, sheriff. We're riding the line looking for work. You know anyone hereabouts who's hiring?"

"You might try asking the No One."

Both cowboys turned to face Jed.

"You're not pulling my leg are you, Sheriff?"

He chuckled. "No, nothing like it, boys. Used to be the B-Bar-M. New owner, Nathan Oliver, bought it last year. Changed the brand to N-O-1. Folks around are starting to call it the No One or Nobody. It's the big spread north of the river. Most of the spreads south of the river are smaller and can't afford to hire. They help each other with round-ups and branding."

"Thanks, Sheriff. We'll ride out there as soon as we finish our drinks."

"See Buster Deets, the foreman. Tell him I sent you. He's a hard man, but fair. If he's hiring, he'll work you hard and pay you well." Touching the brim of his hat, he turned and went back to his table.

"Well, you handled that a lot neater than Alex would have," Neemore said as Jed sat back down.

"I figured them for grub-line riders. They wear their guns too high to be gunslicks and their gear looks like it's been well used. No use prodding a man who's only looking for some beans in his belly."

"Things sure are different around here since you pinned on the badge and got rid of those two stupid deputies."

"Aw, Blythe and Wells weren't bad men,

but after working for Woodbridge, I couldn't rely on 'em. It was time for them to move on."

Neemore finished his beer and stood up. "Time for me to get on home to Josie. We'll pick you and Mrs. Mahan up on the way to the shindig. Josie will be pleased to visit with Gabriella again."

He walked out the back door, pausing to give a longing look toward Ben's Trace. He shook his head sadly at his memories before remembering how much better his relationship with Josie had been since Dolores's untimely death. He shrugged and headed home.

When he finished his beer, Jed made a sweep up one side of the street and down the other, speaking to the few townsfolk who were still about and checking to make sure that the various businesses which were now closed, were locked tight. Rattling the doorknobs was part of the job. On the way back down the street, he saw the Tarrant brothers riding out of town to the north. He hoped Deets had a place for them. It was never pleasant to see a man hungry.

When he got back to Ben's, he turned and crossed to his office. Stepping into the saddle, he tossed a casual wave to Tell and turned his pony toward Gabriella's. They had started building a small ranchhouse out at his place, but until it was finished, they were living at hers. The combined spread placed him among the bigger of the small ranches south of the river. Since they could live on his salary as sheriff, he hadn't sold any cattle except steers and a few culls, preferring to grow their herd. It was more work, but Gabby's cousin Ernesto had come up from Mexico to lend a hand. 'Nesto was a good hand and could handle the day-to-day operations while Jed did his job as sheriff.

Gabby's dogs set up a ruckus as he approached. He knew he'd been recognized when 'Nesto struck a match and lit his *cigarillo* at the corner of the house. Jed smiled. 'Nesto was a good man to have around. He rode straight to the corral and stripped the saddle and bridle off his horse, which immediately lay down and rolled in the dusty dirt. Jed forked some hay over the fence and added enough to make up any shortage Ernesto's horse ate then headed for the house.

Gabby met him on the porch and threw her arms around him. "How was your day?"

"Fine. How was yours? Did little Alex run you ragged?"

"Of course not. He's a good boy. Must take after his daddy. Wash your hands. We have antelope stew and the biscuits are nearly done."

"What? No *tortillas*?" He loved to tease her.

"I thought you'd like the change — but if you prefer *tortillas,* I can make you some."

He laughed. "No, I don't think I could wait."

Gabby went back inside to tend to supper and Jed went to the wash basin on the porch to clean up. Ernesto stepped onto the porch and stood watching him.

"Two riders pass this way *hace un rato.*"

"I figured they would. Couple of grubline riders. I sent them out to the No One to see if Deets can use them."

"*Si. Señor* Deets is hiring. I have heard this."

"Any particular reason?"

Ernesto chuckled. "*Si.* Some of his *caballeros* thought they were too good to dig wells and tanks. *Señor* Deets is not a patient man, so they say."

"Good. Those boys looked like they'd be willing to slop hogs if it got 'em a meal. Sounds like their timing was good."

"*Si.* There is work if they want it." Ernesto put out his smoke and they went inside.

270

Little Alex came running and Jed scooped him up. Sitting at the table, he bounced the toddler on his knee causing him to giggle.

Gabby placed steaming mugs of coffee in front of the seated men followed by a couple big bowls of stew. She returned quickly with a large plate of biscuits covered with a towel and her own bowl of stew.

"Think you'll feel up to going to Nate Oliver's shindig on the Fourth?"

"Feel up to it? I wouldn't miss it."

"Alright. I arranged for your coach today."

"*My* coach?"

"Yes, ma'am. I can't have my wife showing up there horseback like some poor grubline rider looking for a handout, can I?"

"But, a coach?"

"Neemore asked if we'd like to ride out there in Josie's new carryall. I told him that would be nice."

"Oh, it will be. I enjoy talking to Josie. I'm so glad that Mr. Oliver is carrying on the tradition for celebrating Independence Day."

"Me, too. He's turning out to be a fine neighbor. I think we've seen the last of range wars in Callie County."

■ ■ ■ ■

SHE NEVER LIED TO ME

A SHORT STORY

■ ■ ■ ■

A public hanging draws crowds. But looking out of his office window that morning, Sheriff Judson Mahoney knew this event was going to really bring in a lot of fans. He guessed part of the sexiness of this big party was because they were hanging a woman.

No woman had ever been legally hung in New Mexico up until then. There had been some women hung before, but vigilantes did those executions without a judge. But Rio Sanchez County was going to be the first one to do it, and Plaza was the county seat.

No one appeared to want to miss seeing her put to death.

Rumors were all over that her former lover, Randolph Vincentia, would raid the town and stop it happening. But Judson figured Vincentia wasn't that infatuated with her to try and bust her out with all these onlookers to stop him. Besides there were prettier, younger *putas* in the *cantinas* below the border he could have for his own — why risk anything? There were plenty more he could summon with a whistle.

Judson considered him full of bullshit, a bully, and a loud mouth braggart. But there were lots of them below the border and some even in his county a jump north of those lower counties on the border. He had a population of miners, cattle ranchers, and small farmers on places fed by artisan wells at the base of the Sangre de Cristo Mountains. An unusually quiet group that minded their own business and he had a minimal amount of criminal activity in his borders.

In the past two years, he'd sent two rustlers and three stage robbers who'd shot a guard to the gallows. Another man who'd murdered his in-laws for supposedly interfering with his marriage got off after five years' prison time without being hung. The rest of his arrests were drunks, small thieves or wife-beaters.

It all started in a saloon in a crossroads place in the south part called Adobe Sink. Her name was Chrystal Morales, and she came up there from Juarez and made herself available to Alan Stenchcomb. He was a widower with several large ranches. He was in late forties, and this dark-eyed beauty was cute enough to make any red-blooded man excited.

Judson understood she'd worked in the prostitution game since she was twelve on the border. It was, at the time, legal in both New Mexico and across the border in Mexico. There was no limit on going back and forth down there over the international line unless you had gold or silver — then you owed a tariff. There was no penalty for a citizen of either country to work on either side.

While Chrystal had another name on her birth certificate — if there ever was one — that was the title she'd used in Adobe Sink. Some madam had taken her under her wing when she was a teen, seeing Chrystal as a possible big score maker. Most teenaged whores saved up enough money over one or two years at the trade to go back to the home village and buy a *jackal,* and many of those went back pregnant. They married some old boyfriend, confessed their sins to the village priest, and were excused from their actions to live happily ever after.

In Chrystal's case, she must have gone through some classes on how to seduce a man, how to handle them, and then bleed them to death — perhaps it was breed them to death.

After her trial, Judson asked her about her

relationship with Stenchcomb. The two of them played cards for matches in her cell. In those games, he got real acquainted with her and could see just what the late rancher saw in this flirty, dark-eyed lady.

"They told me I could catch him. The woman — his wife — had been dead for over a year."

He waited for her to continue during one of their long private card games.

"They told me to marry him. That was before I agreed to come up here and, as you say, seduce him. You savvy?"

"Yep. I have two queens."

She tossed her hand in. "If you weren't a sheriff, I'd accuse you of cheating."

He laughed. She had the qualities to seduce any man. "Did they clean you up before you came up there?"

"Oh, yes. To get free is very painful business, but they said you must not have any disease to make him dump you. I'm still free today." She offered that to him with a pause until he shook his head to decline her subtle offer.

"I would not have gone through that treatment that doctor gave me if I knew how much it would hurt me."

"Eventually it would have killed you?"

"Maybe, maybe not. I've known sixty-year-old *putas* had it all their lives. I've also known virgins got it and died in two years. This is a tough business."

"How many cards?"

"Two."

"So how did you seduce him?"

"I met him. He asked what I charged. I played hard to get, and he told me if I fit he'd take me home."

"Of course you fit?"

She nodded. By the face she made, he could tell his three fours had just won him even more matches.

"Oh, he was a wonderful lover. I worried he might'a caught the clap before I came to him — he told me if I gave him the clap he'd kill me. But neither of us had it, and that really endeared him to me. We went to Santa Fe and had a lovely honeymoon. He offered to marry me, but he would not marry me in the Catholic Church. He did not trust it. So I lived there for over a year. He made me pregnant once — I shed it."

"Why?"

"I couldn't have a baby for man I knew they might murder, carry that burden along for the rest of my life."

"I see."

"They also told me I must marry him to collect his estate."

"They heard that he had lots of money, property, big loans at high interest made to rich people."

"Oh, I saw that. Now his worthless son will get it all. Millions really. He'll spill it away. He has no brains."

"And you were riding this for your part."

"Oh, he treated me like a wife. I was fine. They got impatient and wanted to kill him, take what they could from the safe, and run to South America."

"They got away with around a half-million dollars. Why didn't you go when you had a chance?"

She shook her head. "Why would they keep me? They killed him, and had the money. Why, at sea they'd just cut my throat and throw me to those fish that eat people. What d'you call them?"

"Sharks."

"Yes. My life wasn't worth ten cents to them. That was the cold hard facts I realized when they fled for Mexico and escaped arrest. They no longer needed me alive either."

"Left you to face the charges?"

"Yes. I can die, and who will miss me?" She shrugged.

"I won't have a card player."

She laughed. "Oh, someone else will lose to you."

"I don't cheat at cards."

"I know. You know now how those two bastards sweet-talked this dumb puta into doing this?"

"Howard Riddle and Koobie Nickels."

"Yes. I would pay you fifty thousand dollars to send them to hell for me. But please whisper at the last moment that Chrystal sends her love and goodbye just before you kill them."

"I swear I will go to South America and dispose of them to earn it."

In a whisper, she said, "I know if you promise me to do it, you will. Then I'll give you the secret to all that gold."

"Trust me?"

"Will you?"

"I promise you I will send them to hell."

"Bring a pen and paper next time you come. I'll draw you a map."

He agreed and left her in the private, thick-walled cell where no one could see or hear her. Next, he locked her door, then unlocked the second one and went into the jail to his office.

The very next question was how had she gotten that much gold? Was it Stenchcomb's? She was too serious about eliminating them to lie to him. He'd have no obligation if it weren't there. He still had a few weeks to decide.

"You win all her matches tonight?" his night jailer, Joe Blocker, asked.

"She may be good-looking, but she isn't a good gambler." He put back the jail keys on the rack and then strapped on his gun.

"Kinda bad, ain't it?"

"I ain't the judge or the jury."

"I can think of a dozen ugly bitches I'd hang before her." Joe shook his head, and Judson headed for the door.

"You ain't the judge, neither," he said over his shoulder.

She wasn't stupid, he'd give her that. After those two bandits had taken her in, Chrystal had known that when they were through with Stenchcomb, they'd eliminate her, too. So there had been no way for her to get out of it.

She drew him the map the next day. He knew where the old ranch was that she'd mentioned and found it easily. A few hours digging and he found three buried strongboxes too, all three heavier than hell. He drug one out and wrestled it open. Chrystal hadn't been lying. It was filled to bursting with gold bars, gleaming in the sun. He'd need a wagon and some help to haul it away.

Whose was it? How had she known about it? No telling.

His buddy Hal Weathers would help him recover it and keep his mouth shut. No way to know how much there was. More than enough to last him and Hal for a lifetime, though. Of that much, he was sure.

The next day, they loaded the three unmarked boxes, covered them with a canvas tarp, and took them out to Hal's place for safekeeping. Jud headed back to town and to play another game of cards with Chrystal.

"I don't want some judge to swap this sentence for a hundred years in jail."

He nodded. He'd heard her.

"There was a reporter guy here today, told me I didn't have to die. I didn't want my body eaten by sharks, but I don't want to rot away the years in some prison, neither. Be certain they hang me. Please."

"Anything else?"

"Some whisky so I don't make a fool of myself. I guess I'm just wishing — but I'd like a real man to make love to me one more time. They've been pleasing me since I was thirteen years old. Hell, they pleased me and I pleased them."

"Might be tough request to fill, but I'll see what I can do. Before anything else, though . . . that thing you put on the map. Does it have an owner I'm going to have to worry about?"

"Nope. I hope that's enough to settle my deal."

"It is. And like I said, I'll try on the other."

She proudly showed him her cards. "Three queens. I finally beat you."

"I won't be your executioner. The state's sending an expert from Santa Fe. You want any special food before it happens?"

"No. Just the whisky that'll help me get there."

"Chrystal, I'll pray for you."

"I should'a met you in my teens. You've made these days precious."

He reached over and blotted her tears with his kerchief. It might never have worked between them, but he agreed. They should have met sooner.

Jud estimated over a thousand people were at her execution. The man they send did a perfect job. Her neck snapped, and she hung numb. They cut her down and Doc formally announced the lady outlaw, Chrystal, was dead.

Some unnamed person had bought her a gravesite, so she was buried in the Methodist cemetery and prayed over at services attended by some hundred people who wished to see the first woman criminal put away.

Judson turned in his badge two weeks

later. The governor appointed another man to the post, Calvin Salazar. Jud took him out to dinner at the saloon the night he arrived in town.

"Was hanging her that tough?"

"I never argued in her favor. She was an accomplice. But she didn't kill him. She simply got in too deep to back out."

"It was them who kilt him, then?"

"Yes."

"They took the money and fled. Didn't even spend a dime on her defense?"

"Not a dime."

"They got away with over two hundred thousand, huh?"

"They say so. I never saw a tally."

"When the governor invited me to Santa Fe, I couldn't believe it was you I was replacing. But I knew it was her that caused you to resign."

"Well you have the keys. It's a quiet place and my men are all dependable. Good luck, Calvin."

They shook hands as friends, and Judson rode back to Hal Weathers's place. They drank some whisky and laid their plans. There were only rumors about where to find Howard Riddle and Koobie Nickels. Some said New Orleans.

"That's where we start," Judson said.

They boarded the train to Fort Worth, then changed trains twice and arrived in the land of Mardi Gras. They took their time there, sampling the local Cajun crawfish and oysters and just trying to blend in. Eventually, they greased enough palms that a shifty, broken-down old dockworker finally told them Riddle and Nickels had sailed off to Brazil.

Booking passage on an ocean liner, they set out for Sao Paulo. Rich Americans in Brazil? Judson thought they'd be easy to find, and he was right. Portuguese is not border Spanish, and English-speakers stick out like a sore thumb. Once they arrived, they learned that Riddle and Nickels had split. Riddle, it turned out, had gone up the Amazon looking for gold. They'd go after him first.

They hired a steam-driven paddle wheel boat for five hundred dollars. The Captain, Ruff McDaniel, a Scotch-Irish expat, studied the pictures of Riddle and told them they'd have no problem finding him upstream.

So they steamed up the huge, muddy river lined with dense jungle and screaming monkeys and noisy birds. A week later, the captain offered to pay for some young *putas* for them at some dingy port where they stopped for wood to fire the steam boiler. Both men declined, but McDaniel had something else for them, though. While he'd been playing with the whores, he'd learned where Riddle had holed up.

"Sounds great. When will we be there?"

"Oh, take us about a week or so."

"If you have him as a prisoner in seven days, we'll pay you five hundred more dollars," Judson said.

McDaniel removed his captain's cap and swept a hand his graying black hair. "You'll have him before then. I promise you."

"Hey, wow can you tell when those fish you spoke about are in the water? What's did you call them?" Hal asked.

"*Piranha.* Throw a cur dog overboard. They'll be there and his life will be short. This river is alive with them."

"That is interesting," Jud said.

"Let's get this over then," Hal said.

"Aye, he'll be here on deck with us shortly."

They toasted each other with their drinks and lay back in the reclining canvas chairs while the boat went full steam ahead upstream. McDaniel had four huge African deckhands that loaded on the wood and fed the boiler. One of them, a man called Chad, could even speak English. He brought them drinks and food, and secured pure spring water for the crew and passengers to drink when they stopped. He did a good job, too. None of them had come down with diarrhea since they'd set out. In addition, Chad had memorized the photos of Riddle and could recognize him on sight.

"You were a sheriff in New Mexico? Are you here for a criminal, sir?" McDaniel asked him one evening at supper.

"The man we seek let a poor woman hang after they forced her to help them kill her man."

"He let them hang her for their crime."

"That's right."

"Oh, that man deserves no mercy."

"No mercy," Judson agreed.

Three nights later, they stopped at another landing. McDaniel's men loaded wood, but the captain informed them they would have further business soon.

"Supper will be late." The captain lowered his voice. "Riddle's here and we'll invite him on board after dark. Be armed — he may have bodyguards. I think we can handle them, but the natives might try to save him since he's been paying them."

"We'll be prepared," Jud told him.

"What do you think?" Hal asked after McDaniel left them,

"Chrystal, where ever you are, I hope you're looking down on us. Tonight Riddle will join the piranha in the muddy water here."

"Think she'll know?"

"She'll know. We'll finally have her half-even with them devils."

A half hour later, two of McDaniel's men brought the fat, half-naked man on board the boat. He was tied up and gagged, and the light from the cabin lamp showed they'd brought them the right man.

Jud nodded. "Ungag him."

They did so.

"Who are you? What do you want me for? Are you crazy? I can pay you. He took all my money from my safe." He meant their captain.

"You know they hung Chrystal Morales?"

"Yeah. She was nothing but a border whore. She killed him."

This made Jud angry. She hadn't killed him, they had. And they'd planned on killing her, too. "Hal, throw something bloody overboard. I want to be sure those fish are ready for this bastard."

"You can't do that!"

"Chrystal wanted you to know she planned this bath for you, Riddle. May God save your soul. Throw him in. I can see those fish down there. If he survives them, I'll shoot him."

His ear-shattering screams only lasted a few minutes before he disappeared under the roiling surface of the Amazon.

Hal nodded with satisfaction. "Supper's ready."

"Good." Jud looked up to the heavens. "Half-done, Chrystal."

After they'd finished eating, Captain McDaniel brought in a huge suitcase stuffed with Riddle's money. One of his resident giants carried it in on his shoulder.

"Did he disappear? For good?"

"Yep." Jud nodded. "And since he'll have no use for money in Hell, we can split this mess up between us."

"Only if you let me and my men help you apprehend the other man."

"We heard a rumor he's in Uruguay."

"Yes, he told us that, too, when we trussed him up. After we get back to the coast, I can have him pinpointed in a week."

"Let's do it, Jud," Hal said, "My feet itch to be back in New Mexico as soon as possible."

"You have a deal, *El Capitan.*" They shook hands on it.

Altogether, the money in the suitcase totalled over two hundred thousand dollars.

They spent the next several days counting it out and splitting it up between them.

Once back in the capital, they went to the bank and rented a couple of safe deposit boxes to keep their money in. Hal and Jud stayed in a luxury hotel while McDaniel ran down the whereabouts of Koobie Nickels.

They were in the bar when the captain joined them, now wearing a spotless white sailor outfit.

"Gentlemen, our man is down on the southern Brazil border. My sources say he has a large estate he bought and some ladies to cover his needs. Shall we take a train down there and handle it?"

"Ready to take a choo-choo south, Hal?"

"I'm ready to go home. Let's go and get this over with."

The train was slow, and an old lady with a goat tried to talk to them like a great seducer of men. Between the language barrier and Hal trying desperately to be polite to her, Jud had a hard time not laughing.

Four days and many stops for firewood later, they bought some horses. There were seven of them, counting the captain's four black men, who were in charge of covering and protecting them. The Brazilian ponies were tough, but small. McDaniel's boys had to hold their bare feet up to ride their mounts.

They approached the area where Koobie Nickels resided. The captain's men scouted the place and scoffed at the lack of security. But the captain mentioned seeing a massive horned bull that came from India.

"He's a sacred bull from India. A Brahma. He hates people. Strange, I know, but I have been to New Delhi and those cattle walk around with people. This bull must have been mistreated when they shipped him over."

"What are you thinking?" Jud asked.

The captain smiled. "He might take the place of the piranha this time?"

Jud turned to Hal. "What do you think?"

His friend wiped sweat from his brow. "Sounds super. Feed him to a bull. Good idea. As if this trip could get any stranger."

"We'll need to get whatever money he has left," the captain reminded them.

"Fine, fifty-fifty." Jud swatted at a bug. He was ready to get back to New Mexico, too. Bugs, flies, monkeys and screaming parrots — he was ready for some dust devils.

McDaniel came up with a fake sales pitch about gold up the Amazon River. He knocked on the front door and told Nickels he needed a backer. It must have worked, because when Chad escorted them to the ranch, they found Nickels tied up in a chair, his new safe empty, and his money packed neatly in two shiny, alligator-skin suitcases.

Jud told them to remove the gag. "You remember Chrystal Morales?"

"You sons o' bitches turn me loose." Nickles went on, swearing and rambling about the violence he would pour down on them.

"She wants you to join her in Hell."

"That *bitch* —"

Jud smashed him in the face with his fist. "No, she was an angel compared to you. You tricked her into taking the blame for the murder. Remember that while you bull is tearing you to pieces. Remember the lady you tricked into setting Stenchcomb up before you left her to hang." None of it mattered to the man. His anger rose until he struck the cussing Nickels in the face again, breaking his nose. "Take him to his fate."

The bull was baited from one pen to another. Still bound in his chair, two of McDaniel's men carried him to the center of the first pen and set him down. Jud would never forgot how the Chad had made a formal bow, asking him in Spanish, "*Matador* are you ready for your *torro*?"

"No! Please! I'll do anything?"

The gate was thrown open, and the massive bull came on the run. Nickels did not scream for long after being tossed six feet in the air by the animal's first charge. He crashed to the ground, only to have one of those sharp horns pierce him through the chest. Scarlet blood squirted out all over the once snow-white sacred bull's head.

They'd done what they'd come to do. Jud was ready to go home. And this time, they'd be sailing first class. Hal was only to happy to agree.

With the thanks of the now-rich Captain McDaniel, they had their newly-made money shipped back home in strong boxes under guard. It cost more to insure that way, but Jud wasn't taking any chances. All told, it came to over four hundred thousand dollars in U.S. currency once they'd had all the foreign bills changed over.

Jud and Hal steamed into south Texas at Galveston after seven long, seasick weeks at sea. Taking both train and stage, they arrived home many thousands of dollars better off than when they left. Three weeks later, their Brazilian-earned money followed, delivered to the Texas State Bank in Austin with little publicity, where it was stored in the vault.

There was much to do. Jud and Hal enlarged their ranch's land holdings considerably, as well as the number of cows in their herd. Jud started construction of new, sprawling ranchhouse.

In town, two churches and one parsonage received a new tin roofs. The Catholic Church's fund for the poor grew so large that none of the little naked children in Rio Sanchez County ever went to bed hungry again. Doc acquired some new medical items only big town doctors could afford, and several of the town's widow women had their tabs at the mercantile paid off by an unknown hand.

Jud courted Julie, a twenty-some year old dark-eyed widow without children whose husband had died a year ago in a horse wreck. She accepted a position as his house-keeper in their much larger new *casa.* He promised that if she were to become pregnant, he'd marry her.

Jud and Hal were seated comfortably in the shade one day drinking some *olla*-cooled tea under the shade and conversing about their recent world tour.

"Well that settled the Chrystal's deal. Are you happy to have it over?"

Jud nodded. "Yep. Glad to be home."

"I expect she was pretty honest with you."

"I didn't really believe her when she told me she'd been cured of any diseases before she joined Stenchcomb."

"You're talking about her being over the clap?"

"Yes, she said she didn't have it. That she'd been cured."

Hal sat up straight. "You mean you — ?"

"Yep." Jud smiled. "But she never lied to me."

ABOUT THE AUTHOR

Dusty Richards grew up riding horses and watching his western heroes on the big screen. He even wrote book reports for his classmates, making up westerns since English teachers didn't read that kind of book. His mother, though, didn't want him to be a cowboy, so he went to college, then worked for Tyson Foods and auctioned cattle when he wasn't an anchor on television. His lifelong dream, though, was to write the novels he loved. He sat on the stoop of Zane Grey's cabin and promised he'd one day get published, as well. In 1992, that promise became a reality when his first book, *Noble's Way,* hit the shelves. In the years since, he's published over 160 more, winning nearly every major award for western literature along the way. His 150th novel, *The Mustanger and the Lady,* was adapted for the silver screen and released as the motion picture *Painted Woman* in 2017.

Sadly, Dusty passed away in early 2018, leaving behind a legion of fans and a legacy of great western writing that will live on for generations.

The employees of Thorndike Press hope you have enjoyed this Large Print book. All our Thorndike Large Print titles are designed for easy reading, and all our books are made to last. Other Thorndike Press Large Print books are available at your library, through selected bookstores, or directly from us.

For information about titles, please call:
  (800) 223-1244

or visit our website at:
  gale.com/thorndike

Printed in the USA
CPSIA information can be obtained
at www.ICGtesting.com
JSHW021124030924
69072JS00006B/6